The Gnashvine

The Gnashvine

Cover Design by John Hackett
Interior Typesetting by Melissa Williams Design

Published in the United States by Tyler H. Jolley

ISBN: 978-1-958734-32-2 (paperback)
ISBN: 978-1-958734-33-9 (hardcover)
ISBN: 978-1-958734-34-6 (eBook)

The Gnashvine

Tyler H. Jolley

Jack Neal Booth

This is dedicated to my dad,
for teaching me how to plant
and take care of a garden.

ONE:

The Avling Universal Crop Vault—AUCV—nearly blended in with the mountain. With its minimalistic light-gray ramped entrance to a single outbuilding that was constructed out of local shale, it was hard to spot from the ground and even harder from the air. It had been designed this way, though Antarctica's permanent white landscape mixed with constant snowfall had washed away any color.

The vault had been built into the side of the mountain to the depth of permafrost. Once inside, one would observe that most tunnel walls and the seed vaults themselves were all constructed directly into the permafrost plug. The design was deliberate, functioning to keep the environment cold year-round with slight temperature fluctuation. This, in turn, created a perfect place for seeds to stay dormant, denying them any opportunity to sprout. In addition, the space provided excellent conditions to experiment with genetically altered plants that could grow in freezing temperatures. At least, that's what Jørn had been told. Confirming this information was nearly impossible, as the AUCV was notoriously secretive.

The helicopter that Jørn found himself in was warm, but he shivered. The excitement had boiled over, and his left leg bounced like a young boy on his way to see the newest blockbuster movie that he'd been waiting for over two years to come out. He stared at a blinking red light in the sea of colorful ones on the helicopter's control panel. Coiled pale-yellow communication wires hung from the ceiling and attached to headphones, which the three occupants wore.

Next to him, Elinor sat calmly, combing her fingers through her blonde hair, staring out the window. She was the love of his life, but she didn't know that. Elinor looked warm and comfortable, and Jørn fought the urge to snuggle up against her. In his mind, she wouldn't find this repulsive, just unprofessional. After all, they were invited here by the prestigious higher-ups on the board of the AUCV.

The view outside drove his constant need to shiver. Snow-covered mountain peaks void of foliage sloped into a frozen lake to the left. He slipped his legs into a green snowsuit as they started their descent. The cramped space in the helicopter made it difficult to finish dressing in the AUCV-assigned snowsuit made for subzero temperatures. He would have to wait until landing to finish donning it.

Elinor pointed at her window, her voice-activated headphones crackling to life. "I think I see it!"

Jørn turned to look at what she was pointing at since he had only seen the AUCV in photos. A blocky gray entrance protruded from the base of a smaller peaked mountain like a frost-bitten nose on an old Scandinavian man.

It was difficult for Jørn to look past Elli's beauty though. The hammering heart in his chest was almost too much as he watched her perfect jawline as she smiled with her observation. Elinor, or Elli, was the most beautiful girl Jørn had ever seen. Every time she looked at him, her blue eyes drowned him in their depths. In the past he had learned not to stare, sometimes resorting to just shaking his head violently when he realized he was looking too long. She had asked why and he would blame an itch or some other pathetic reason. Spending most of her time studying seeds indoors kept her skin healthy and milky-smooth, like the latex substance found in milkweed when broken open.

She pressed her unblemished forehead against the helicopter's window, peering through the flurry of snow. Like Jørn, she had pulled her green snowsuit on only half-way. She wore a tight black long-sleeved undergarment underneath, accentuating perfect curves that would make Michelangelo proud.

The tone of her voice was surprisingly clear in Jørn's headset. "Can you believe it?" She sounded giddy.

"No! I can't *be-leaf* it!"

"What?"

"No. I can't *be-leaf* it, I said."

He heard her groan. "Plant puns again, Jørn?" She smiled.

He fidgeted with the thumb-wide black zipper of his snowsuit, happy she appreciated his nerdiness.

"You're lucky this trip panned out," the pilot said. He didn't look at them, but he'd obviously heard all of their conversation. "Normally, the weather's too rough this time of year, and it's impossible to land, but it looks like fate has called you here."

Fate.

The word was so foreign to Jørn. He knew what it meant, of course, but he wasn't sure he believed in such a thing.

"When's the next trip planned?" Elli asked.

"A month from now," the pilot said. "Don't worry, though. If there's a major emergency, you can contact us, and we'll do our best to get out here as quick as possible. But a two-day snowmobile trip might be the only option, weather depending."

What could happen? Jørn thought. *We're only dealing with seeds and harmless plants.*

Elli squirmed, biting her lip and trying to hide the very *obvious* smile on her face. She could barely contain her excitement. Jørn understood how she felt—it was a huge opportunity to be able to study at the AUCV. They'd both been selected out of hundreds of applicants.

"Landing now," the pilot said. "There's a narrow platform jutting out from the vault's entrance. It *will* be a tight landing, but don't panic. I've done this before."

"That's reassuring," Elli whispered.

"I'll try my hardest not to *soil* myself," Jørn said. This got him a blank stare from Elli and silence from both her and the pilot.

"Anyway," she said, "what are you most excited for, Jørn?"

For a split moment, Jørn almost told her the truth: He was most excited to spend the next two months with her. But he caught himself at the last moment.

"I don't know," he said.

She shot him a confused look and then answered her own question. "I'm most excited to see what's inside the vault. Very little is known about it. Did you know that? Of course you did. Well, I should say, very little is *publicly* known about it. As far as I'm aware, there are no photos of the labs inside, just the seeds and the plants they have stored."

She spoke so fast that it sounded like the helicopter's rotor blades were forcing the words out of her.

"Every genus of plant is stored in there. Every seed that's ever been discovered in the world, and probably

4

even more than that, exists behind those steel doors. And so few people have seen it with their own eyes. I mean, probably less than a few dozen grad students in total have had the opportunity to work in there. And we're now two of those people."

She relaxed back in her chair, probably exhausted from her monologue, and the pilot chuckled faintly. "It's like Charlie getting the golden ticket to the chocolate factory."

Pressing his back into the seat, Jørn mustered enough courage to ask, "So you don't believe the rumors?"

"That a secret world government is using that story as a cover to actually store weapons of mass destruction?" Elli raised her eyebrows at him. "Of course not. I'm a scientist, not a moron." She paused then, as if it had just occurred to her, and slowly turned back to him. "Do *you* believe those rumors?"

"Not those rumors, no," Jørn said. Then, realizing how he had answered the question, he had the sudden, overpowering urge to kick himself.

Elli shifted in her seat to face him. As she did, a swath of fruity perfume drifted past Jørn. He felt his knees go weak.

"What rumors are you talking about, then, Jørn?"

He fidgeted, hoping she'd suddenly drop the subject, but she didn't.

"There are rumors that high-energy cosmic rays hit the Earth in the exact spot this vault is built," he said. She tilted her head at him, implying that she knew that wasn't the end to the theory. He gulped, continuing. "Some people think these rays brought extraterrestrial life to our Earth and it's just an Area 51 in the snow."

"Here we go," the pilot said, interrupting him.

Elli turned to face her window without responding,

and Jørn looked out of his. Sometimes she was outright dismissive of him—it almost made him question of they were right for each other. *Almost.*

The craggy mountain peak appeared so close now. Gray rock peeked through hardened snow, much like the looming steel vault doors below.

The pilot steered the helicopter until it was dangerously close to the mountainside. Next to him, Jørn could feel Elli's nervousness. She seemed to vibrate all over with anxiety and cringed away from the mountainside as if her shifting that little bit would keep the helicopter from crashing against it. But he knew the pilot was in control.

Slowly, they descended alongside the cliff face. Below them, a thin platform rose from the swirling vortex of snow. And then, before Jørn could even blink, they were on the ground.

"Let's suit up," Elli said, completely forgetting that she'd been afraid a moment before.

TWO:

The green snowsuits had two zippers—one running up the middle of the chest and another running up the middle of the back that eventually joined together a tightly-fitted hood. It was near impossible to put on alone.

The helicopter stayed sealed shut until they were fully dressed. Jørn was grateful for this. He didn't want to face the frigid temperatures quite yet.

"Here," Elli said, stepping up behind him, "let me help you." She zipped him up from the back. Once it reached his head, she grabbed his hand and spun him around. He ignored the flaring excitement in his stomach.

She turned around, and he reached for her zipper. She'd taken off her shirt and stuffed it into her bag so she would have something dry and clean to wear once they entered the vault. He averted his eyes from her bra and bare back, then zipped her up quickly, trying to steady his shaking hands.

"Thanks," she muttered once he pulled away.

Jørn strapped on his goggles, fitted his gloves, and ensured Elli had done the same.

The pilot spun in his seat and shot them a thumbs-up. They returned the gesture with thick gloved thumbs and goofy grins. Their internship had begun. The pilot pressed one of the countless buttons on his dashboard. Something inside the cabin hissed, and then the door handle clicked.

Jørn picked up his bag of belongings, and Elli did the same. They were fairly large, containing only clothes and a few personal items—most everything else would be provided inside the vault.

Jørn grabbed the handle, twisted it, and yanked open the door. An icy blast of biting air and crystals of snow slammed into them, and he immediately swore. He'd always hated the cold. It's why he'd become a botanist with an emphasis on mechanobiology in the first place— most plants couldn't grow in freezing temperatures, which meant he should have never had to enter areas of freezing temperature. And yet here he was.

With their bags unloaded, they jumped out of the helicopter, and Jørn shut the door. The rotor blades still spun, whipping up the crystalline snow chunks around them. Nothing but white clouded his vision. He could barely make out Elli crouching to avoid the blades. He followed suit. Together, they waited for the helicopter to lift off and be swallowed by the gray skies.

Once the torrent of snow had subsided, the two students stood, emerging on the landing pad like sprouts piercing moist fertilized soil in the spring. The snow settled, and the door to the vault came into view. Jørn dusted himself off, but Elli took off immediately, clapping her gloved hands and shouting in excitement. He followed her. He couldn't wait to get out of the cold and see what amazing botany phenomena was happening behind those doors.

There was a small slot next to the door protected by a thick layer of plastic. He began patting his pockets for the key card—a habit he had developed from years of working in labs—before realizing he had stored it in his bag. He swung the pack off his shoulders and began rummaging through it.

"We're here," Elli said, voice coming out in frosty plumes. "I can't believe we're here." She reached out and touched the vault doors as if they were the pearly gates. Her breath caught in her throat. She removed her hand, leaving behind a perfect mitten imprint in the frost.

Jørn found the slick white key card with the black magnetic strip on the back, mailed to their department chairman months ago in preparation for this exact moment. His had a grainy photo of his handsome mug on the front, with the words "Student Internship with Avling Universal Crop Vault" in red lettering next to a green-and-blue logo of a globe with a tan seed emerging out of the top of it.

As he tried to insert it, he fumbled with gloved hands and the plastic card slipped and stabbed face up into the snow. Elli tapped the top of her wrist with one finger and smirked.

"I know, I know. I'm trying. These gloves are too bulky. I don't have use of my fingers." Frosted breaths huffed in front of his face, fogging his goggles and blurring his vision.

Using his gloved fingers as nimbly as he could, he retrieved the precious ID, brushed it off, and blew at the remaining flakes of snow before trying to insert it again. Elli waited with one hand on her hip.

There was an audible beep and a green light shined through the hazy, iced-over indicator screen. The doors swung open immediately.

Warmer air wafted over both of them. Jørn shrugged and picked up his bag. He didn't hesitate to look inside before stepping over the threshold. He just wanted to be away from the cold.

Elli squealed in excitement and followed him inside. Jørn turned and pushed a big red button on the other side of the vestibule. The doors sealed closed behind them and they were alone in a temperature-controlled airlock.

Darkness enveloped them before a row of orange sensor lights flickered to life. The bulbs were aged to the point of giving off only a faint glow, but it was better than nothing.

"Isn't someone supposed to meet us here?" Elli asked, glancing around.

They were in an antechamber of sorts.

"They said someone would be here," Jørn said, glancing at his watch, "at *tree* o'clock."

Elli rolled her eyes. "No, Jørn. That one was especially bad."

He chuckled nervously, fiddling with the key card and pacing back and forth. There was a door on the wall in front of them, but it looked like it couldn't be opened from where they were. It was probably a security measure to keep out all the visitors.

"I'm sorry," Elli said, fanning her hand at her face. "Is it just me, or are you blistering in here?"

Jørn didn't answer. How could he be? Aside from the few moments they'd spent outside, he'd always felt too warm and too sweaty around Elli. Today was just like any other day.

She pulled her front zipper down a few inches, revealing some of her skin, then unzipped and removed her hood. Blonde hair spilled out to her shoulders, and she shook it out, running her fingers through it.

Then she looked at Jørn.

He looked away.

"Do you hear that?" Elli asked, pressing her ear against the wall, ignoring their awkward eye contact.

Jørn followed suit, listening for any sounds out of the ordinary. At first, he heard some sort of ruckus, like a bunch of metal shelves falling over all at once, but then he recognized what it was.

"*Back in Black*," Jørn said, shaking his head.

"They're blasting old rock and roll?" Elli asked. "Isn't it supposed to be, like, a professional lab in there or something? Why are they playing music?" She pressed her face harder against the door. "And why so *loud*?"

At that moment, the doors began sliding open. Elli jumped back and hurriedly composed herself. Jørn simply remained where he was.

High-powered fluorescent lights spilled through the opening door and into the antechamber, and Elli gasped when a long corridor of glass walls appeared.

"Welcome," said a strangely tan man, stepping into view, "to the Avling Universal Crop Vault."

THREE:

"I'm Salomon," the man said. "I'm what you'd call the head honcho of this place." He held out his arms as if the corridor were something impressive. Apparently, Elli thought it was, however, because she grinned ear to ear.

"You two must be Jørn and Elinor." He beckoned them out of the antechamber. The rock music had stopped the moment the doors opened. Jørn wondered when it'd start to play again.

They followed the tall, lanky man into the main hallway. His stature was somewhere in between emaciated and fit. His skin had a well-tinted tan for being in a cave for long periods of time. His white beard was well-trimmed and hung no more than an inch from a long jawline, and his hair was long enough to almost touch his shoulders. Striking blue eyes gave them a once over as he rubbed his bearded chin.

"Yes," Elli said. "I'm Elli, this is Jørn. Listen, Dr. Salomon, we're—"

"No 'doctor' title, please," Salomon said, waving his hand. "We're all friends here. Except, on second thought, you should probably refer to Dr. Miller as Doctor. He seems to have an aversion to being called something different."

Unsure what to do or say, Jørn turned his attention to

Elli. She had more questions than someone could reasonably answer in one day, and he knew he could rely on her for new conversation topics.

"When will we be meeting the other doctors?" she asked.

"In due time," Salomon said. "I asked them here today, but they're all too busy with projects at the moment. No doubt, you'll meet all of them soon enough."

"Our instructions weren't very clear for what to do once we got here," Elli said.

Salomon laughed. "Oh yes, of course. Well, I'll take you on a tour of the place now, if you want, and then you have the day to get settled. Tomorrow, we'll put you to work."

Jørn wasn't sure how to feel. He'd been pleasantly surprised to land this position, and a part of him had been excited to spend two months in such a prestigious lab—and of course, he'd been elated to discover Elli would be accompanying him—but now that he was here, he felt weird. They were essentially sealed within this vault for two months with no way off the continent, and stuck with a bunch of strangers.

"You can leave your bags here," Salomon said, pointing at the ground. "We have a janitor desperate for something to clean up besides dirt and pollen. He'll take them down to the sleeping berths."

Elli laughed. Jørn didn't. They both dropped their bags.

"This is the main room," Salomon said as they headed down the corridor to the right. "On either side, you'll see the storage facilities where extra supplies are kept." Behind the glass walls were rows of boxes, cases, and crates. "We store them near the front because the deeper we get into the mountain, the more stable we can keep the temperature, and we prefer to use the space back there to store our seeds and plants."

They exited the corridor and found themselves in a vast, empty area. Two staircases led to the same walkway that branched off into separate hallways. At the far end was the cafeteria, where someone sat with their back turned, eating off an orange tray.

The cafeteria was a carved-out room with white permafrost walls, lined with blue barrels for water and kraft-colored barrels with food.

"Hi, I'm Jørn." He waved, but the man didn't turn and acknowledge him.

"Friendly," Elli said sarcastically.

"You'll find there are many introverts here. Not only that, people rarely stay long, so some find it not worth their time to make fleeting friendships. As I was saying, to the left"—Salomon pointed to the left staircase—"you'll find where we store plants and seeds. To the right is where the labs are located. Which would you like to see first?"

"The labs," Jørn and Elli said in unison. Salomon smiled and led them up the right staircase. Once they reached the top, they all turned around. Somebody was running down the grated walkway, their footsteps ringing through the main room like fallen cymbals clattering on the ground.

A young man ran toward them. He was overweight, but looked to be in much better shape than Jørn felt because the guy wasn't breaking a sweat despite running.

"Ah, Goran," Salomon said.

Goran slowed to a stop and glanced worriedly at Salomon.

"Goran, these are the new interns I told everyone about—Jørn and Elli. Jørn and Elli, this is Goran, one of our permanent seed techs."

Jørn shook Goran's outstretched hand, and Elli followed suit. "Nice to meet you both," he said, flashing them a quick smile.

"Salomon," Goran said, shifting all of his attention to the chief doctor, "can I talk to you for a moment?"

"We can speak in front of them," Salomon said, jamming his thumb in Jørn and Elli's direction.

Goran sighed, scratched the back of his head, then leaned up and whispered something in Salomon's ear. Concern flashed across Salomon's face, but that concern quickly became curiosity.

"What do you think it is?" Elli whispered, leaning in to Jørn.

He felt like his knees had turned to rubber. She was so close that he could feel her breath on his neck.

"Not sure," he said, surprised he didn't stumble. "Judging by how nervous Goran is, seems like it could be an accident of sorts."

"I agree," Elli said.

Salomon whispered something back to Goran, who nodded and took off in the direction he'd come.

"Sorry about that," Salomon said. "Goran can be a bit strange, especially around new interns. But if you'd like to come see what he was talking about, just follow me. We can finish the tour later."

"What did he tell you?" Elli asked as they headed in the same direction Goran had gone. Jørn was surprised by her forwardness.

"Apparently, one of the techs found a puddle of blood from an accident yesterday. They claim a plant is now growing in that pool of blood."

Jørn nearly choked. "Are you sure your seed techs are right in the head?" he asked.

"Everyone here is as sane as can be," Salomon said.

"But even then, I must warn you that being locked up in this vault for months at a time will feel as if it will drive you a bit insane."

FOUR:

The actual seed vault that the Avling Universal Crop Vault was famous for was something internally referred to as The Box. It was a legitimate vault built into the mountain—the rest of the AUCV was constructed around it. The Box was designed to store every genus of seed that existed in the world. While the vault was built with research in mind, The Box was a security measure for the world. If ever there were a catastrophic event—dinosaur-extinction-level asteroid, nuclear war, alien invasion—the survivors would still have access to the world's plants.

Personally, Jørn thought that was dramatic reasoning, but many botanists—including himself—needed some extra reasons to get excited about plants, no matter how improbable those reasons were.

Salomon, Jørn, and Elli rushed to the back of the AUCV. The walk to the seed vault was a fast five minutes. They passed rooms and offshoot hallways that housed a library, a lounge full of couches and plush chairs, with a big screen and shelves of DVDs, a laundry room, a medical bay, a weight room, and IT offices.

"Fuel and waste disposal is on the opposite side of the cafeteria near the front," Salomon said as they approached the heavy orange one-foot-thick steel door, supported by arm-thick hinges. "That's the tour in a nut-shell." Salomon came off slightly flustered and rushed.

"One rule here is that if you go into the vault, you have to remove your name tag and hang it from one of these hooks on this board," Salomon said, removing his name tag and placing it on one of ten silver-covered hooks. Goran's name tag was hanging next to his. Some of the less commonly used hooks had frost growing on them.

Entering, Jørn heard two men struggling to lift something heavy. There were grunts, followed by a string of what he could only guess was cussing in a different language. They rounded a corner, and Goran was picking up fallen boxes and replacing the items that had spilled from it, while another seed tech took pictures from every angle of a puddle of blood on the floor.

When Jørn stepped farther into The Box, he shivered. It was significantly colder in here than in the rest of the vault.

"Jørn, Elli, meet Kennet," Salomon said, pointing to the seed tech holding the camera.

"What happened here?" Elli asked, standing next to Jørn.

"Last night," Kennet said, never pulling his eye away from the camera's viewfinder, "the shelf fell over and hit Dr. Miller on the head. He didn't report the accident until this morning. Then we came in here to clean up and found this." He pointed to the center of the puddle staining the snowy floor. "Looks like someone spilled their cherry slushie."

Jørn looked past the crimson stain and crouched down. "Is that a *plant sprout*?" He leaned down closer, squinting his eyes at what appeared to be the green stem of a plant growing straight out of the red puddle.

"Appears so," Kennet said.

"Looks to be some kind of tracheophyte," Jørn said. "A fern, maybe."

"Did Dr. Miller happen to bring any plants in here during his visit last night?" Salomon asked.

"No," Kennet said. "He came to retrieve some basic green plant seeds, but never ended up grabbing them."

Jørn stood up. The blood had dried in the freezing temperatures, and he was getting unpleasant whiffs of copper.

"Just to be clear," Salomon said. "You're hypothesizing that this plant grew overnight in a puddle of blood?"

Kennet took another picture. "Guess so," he said.

How can that be? Jørn thought. *It doesn't make sense. But maybe . . .*

"I suppose this could happen given the nutrient conditions of the blood," he said. "Blood is organic. It has nitrogen, phosphorus, iron, and potassium. Super beneficial for plants." Jørn put his hands in his pocket and paced around the small plant. "I suppose the warm blood melted a little bit of frost to produce water so that the salts could be diluted." He rubbed his chin. "Root burn shouldn't be a problem. But it begs the question of photosynthesis. I don't know how, but it grew."

Goran had finally finished picking up the mess. Jørn got his first real view deep into The Box when he stepped up to the seed tech with the camera. It was endless, stretching into eventual darkness. Hallways branched off in either direction every ten feet. And all along the walls were metal shelves. They were filled with briefcases, metal boxes, glass cases, fridges, terrariums, and containers Jørn didn't recognize. Seeds were everywhere. Stored in drawers, on the shelves, inside all the cases. Some were lying on tables and in cups, and there were even a few scattered on the floor. Everything and every seed was labeled, aside from some clearly misplaced ones.

For the first time since they'd arrived, Jørn's situation finally dawned upon him. He was at the most prestigious scientific institution in the history of the world. Very few people had seen what he was seeing now. He'd confused his indifferent attitude about the AUCV with his feelings of inferiority. He felt out of place, even though, deep down, he knew he had the best research proposal and deserved to be here. Between him and Elli, the thesis committee would have some robust research theses to brag about when they returned. That was the whole reason they were selected to come out here and spend time with Dr. Salomon in the AUCV.

Salomon fell to his stomach and began inspecting the tracheophyte.

"What do you think this is?" Elli asked. She sidled up closer to Jørn, shivering slightly.

"I'm not sure," he said, "but I'm determined to get to the *root* of it."

She stepped away.

"Goran," Salomon said. "Do you have a thermometer?"

Goran shot Salomon an annoyed look, stole a quick glance at Jørn and Elli, and then fished in his pocket. "Laser? Or rectal?"

"Laser," Salomon said. "And I'm not going to ask about the other one."

Goran scoffed. "It fits nicely into a freshly cut stem to take internal temps of plants growing in the greenhouse."

Salomon held out his hand and Goran tossed him the laser thermometer. The lead scientist caught it and pointed it at the plant.

"The Box is kept at a steady three-point-three degrees Celsius," Salomon explained.

The laser temp gauge beeped, and he held it close to his eyes. "Odd."

Before anyone could inquire further, Salomon read the temperature out loud. "Thirty-six-point-eight degrees Celsius."

Nobody spoke. Jørn knew they were all thinking the same thing: that was abnormally hot for a plant. In any other situation, he would have chalked it up to environmental factors, but they were in a temperature-controlled room. The only way it would read the plant's temperature so high was if the thermometer were broken. And somehow, Jørn doubted anyone carried faulty equipment around here.

"Let's leave it here for a moment," Salomon said as he stood. "For now, Goran and Kennet, go inform Dr. Miller of this . . . unusual circumstance. And carefully remove the plant and the blood and bring them to the lab. I think I speak for all of us when I say the idea of studying that thing is thrilling."

Kennet nodded, and Goran merely glowered.

Jørn realized something else that had been bothering him since his arrival. The people here didn't talk like scientists. Everything about them—their mannerisms, attitudes, and dialogue—was relaxed.

"Jørn and Elli," Salomon said, turning to them, "let me give you a more in-depth tour."

They followed him out of The Box—Elli sighing with relief once they escaped the cold. As Salomon led them down the walkway and toward the labs at the other end, Jørn realized he'd once again been wrong about his feelings. He didn't feel indifferent *or* out of place. He felt uneasy. Where that uneasiness stemmed from was a mystery, but it was like everything within his body was on edge, like his heart was hesitant to pump too loudly.

"Do you have the jitters at all?" he asked, whispering the question to Elli.

"Yes," she said. "I am *so* nervous."

He nodded, more to himself than to her. Maybe it was just bad nerves. Maybe he was just too much inside of his own head.

I need some fresh air, he thought, understanding that he was about as far from "fresh air" as one could get.

Before they entered the section of the vault containing the labs—a place Jørn felt he would probably be more at ease—something else occurred to him.

Thirty-six-point-eight degrees Celsius.

It wasn't just the temperature of the strange plant they'd found in the blood.

That was the standard temperature of a human being.

FIVE:

By the time they reached the lab, the revelation about the plant's temperature was gone from Jørn's mind. After they passed through the main room and entered the other side of the vault, Salomon paused at the first door. He had clipped his name badge back onto his shirt.

"Here is the hot greenhouse," he said, pointing to the sign above the door trim that identified it. Before either of them could ask a question, Salomon opened the door and motioned for Elli and then Jørn to go through.

The sign had been accurate. They had entered a greenhouse that looked like any other, with a vaulted ceiling that covered rows and rows of greenery. The only evident difference between this greenhouse and any others was the heat. Panels lined with sunlight bulbs—special lightbulbs that produced enough infrared rays and ultraviolet light to simulate sunlight—blazed down on the plants.

"I've never heard of a hot greenhouse before," Elli said, looking over her shoulder at Salomon, the bright lights drowning out her stunning blue eyes.

He raised his hand, smiling, "Part of the AUCV's duty is to genetically modify every plant we have access to so that each one can survive in any number of harsh environments. This, obviously, was designed to create plants that can survive in intense heat. In the chance that the sun scorches most of the Earth, we have plants that will not only grow in those conditions, but will thrive."

Elli peered closer at a plant with white petals and a yellow carpel. "Sanguinaria canadensis," she said.

"What?" Jørn asked.

"Bloodroot. Used to make some herbal medicines and sometimes red dye." She looked back at Salomon. "That's an odd plant to genetically modify."

"Why?" Jørn asked. He was lost in this conversation. Mechanobiology had very little to do with the purpose of plants and more to do with how the mechanical movements of said plants affected their biology.

"Because it's not very useful," Elli said. "It's not a plant I'd be focused on in the AUCV program."

"Ah," Salomon said, wagging his finger, "you forget we work on *every plant genus*. We did create a rudimentary system that labeled plants on the most objective scale possible from most useful to entirely useless. It is simply, among others, bloodroot's turn in the experiments."

Elli's mouth fell open. "How many plants have you successfully genetically modified?"

"I have no idea," he said. "I'm sure some computer somewhere has some idea, but I'm not sure any of us have consciously kept track. Plenty, I can tell you that. We still have more to go—will for years. But we've made some sizeable progress so far."

"What about cold temperatures?" Elli asked. "You have a hot greenhouse. I assume you have a regular greenhouse. Do you have a cold one too?"

"Absolutely," Salomon said, "it's just out here." He left the hot greenhouse, and Jørn and Elli followed him. They passed a door marked "GREENHOUSE" and came upon another cleverly titled "COLD GREENHOUSE." Salomon pushed the door open.

"Most places here don't have locks," he said. "We encourage collaboration. It'd be dangerous for someone to accidentally get locked in, for example, the hot greenhouse."

"Makes sense," Jørn said, uncomfortable with the thought of being trapped in any room in the vault.

Elli led the way into the cold greenhouse, which was similar to the hot one. Here, the light was tinged with blue, and ice had formed around the boxes and pots the plants grew from.

Yet the sign had been accurate. They had entered a greenhouse that looked like a jungle—another vaulted ceiling covered rows and rows of greenery. The floor was a grid of elevated walkways with water flowing constantly under them. Lily pads, moss, and cattails growing within the depths made the water murky and uninviting. But the noticeable difference between this greenhouse and any others was the lack of heat. Refrigerated coolers lined the roof, pumping out freezing air and coating the plants with a frozen environment. Exposed bulbs were the only source of light, shining down through columns of melted frost.

"All three greenhouses contain the same plants. It's easier to keep track of what seeds we've planted when we ensure we've correctly genetically modified them for all temperatures," Salomon explained.

"Fascinating," Elli said, looking closely at another plant.

"Did you find the environment had much of an effect on how they grew?" Jørn asked.

"Well, yes," Salomon said. "As our visiting mechanobiologist, you should know better than anyone that *everything* about the environment affects the plant. We tend to tinker with their genetics until they grow the same in each environment, but that's why we specifically requested they send someone from your field. We've kept all the data, and we thought not only would it be useful for you and your corner of the scientific world, but we figured you might be able to help us discover how to genetically modify these plants faster. If we can understand exactly what different temperatures do to a plant's biology, then we'd better understand the process we have to change in order to achieve success."

"I love to study the mechanical aspects of biological systems," Jørn said. "Plus, this new interdisciplinary field focuses on understanding how physical forces change the mechanical properties of cells and tissues."

"What were your main focuses?" Salomon asked.

"Forces that impact cellular behaviors, such as cell shape, movement, growth, differentiation, and even how cells communicate with each other. I love that I can combine principles from biology, engineering, and physics to examine how these mechanical forces at the cellular and molecular levels contribute to the function and development of organisms. But I'm open to learning anything that comes my way."

"Very impressive," Salomon said.

"I'm just so grateful I—I mean, *we*—got picked to study under you. As Elli said, this is fascinating."

Salomon grabbed him by the shoulder. A sudden, urgent look entered his eyes. "Never doubt yourself, Jørn. Never doubt yourself. The world, God, science, *something* is always listening to our thoughts. And if you stop believing in yourself, the universe will too."

Jørn fidgeted, unsure how to take the sincerity of Salomon's remark.

"You are an expert on the leading edge of an emerging field. You were chosen to come here for what's in there." He pointed at Jørn's head. "But what you do here, what you're capable of"—he pointed at Jørn's chest—"is right there."

"Uh . . . thanks?" he said uncomfortably.

"Speaking of your potential," Salomon said, "let's go to the labs. I bet both of you want to see where you'll be spending the majority of your time for the next two months."

SIX:

The lab was everything Jørn had imagined it. Glassware sets, machinery, chemical hoods, carts. It was vast and walled off into separate sections. There was no privacy by design—the walls were mostly glass, and every corner was well-lit. A dozen or so seed techs wearing long white coats milled about, carrying trays and samples here and there, slipping panels under microscopes, jotting down notes. Every surface was covered in greenery or seeds, and the entire place smelled like it had been cleaned only moments earlier.

"We opted for one big lab as opposed to a handful of smaller ones," Salomon said. "Saves space, fewer walls and all. And again, it encourages collaboration."

"Excuse us." It was Goran and Kennet, who still had the camera hung around his neck. They moved between Salomon, Jørn, and Elli, carrying the frozen blood and the plant on a tray. Goran once again glared at Jørn and Elli as he passed by.

"Ah," Salomon said, clapping his hands. "Yes! Thank you!" The old man looked around for a moment, searching for a seed tech who wasn't preoccupied before his eyes settled on a girl passing them.

"Asta!" he called.

The girl turned. Her black hair was cut short, making

her green eyes far brighter than they probably were. Her lips were chapped, and she looked extremely disinterested in anything happening around her.

"Dr. Miller had an accident in The Box," Salomon explained. While the scientist, Asta, seemed unimpressed with what he was saying, she was fully attentive. "Goran and Kennet found a plant growing in Dr. Miller's puddle of frozen blood."

At this, Asta raised one eyebrow.

"I would like you to drop what you're doing and study it." He pointed to Goran and Kennet, who was slowly setting the tray down on an empty table.

"As you wish," Asta said. She turned without casting another look and went to the table Goran and Kennet had just left the blood-plant on.

"Can I go with her?" Elli asked. She had that eager look in her eyes again, like she was a starved person, and the science before her was a Thanksgiving feast.

"No need to ask me," Salomon said. "This is your job. As long as you're working, the grant money is happy."

She flashed Salomon a smile, took one last look at Jørn, and then took off after Asta.

"Salomon," Kennet said, appearing behind them. "Thought you'd like to know Dr. Miller is awake. Doc Kincaid still wants to keep him at the infirmary for another day, but figured you'd wanna question him."

"Sure," Salomon said. "Thanks." He looked at Jørn. "I'm not sure if a mechanobiologist will be very useful in questioning Dr. Miller, but do you want to come along?"

Jørn didn't have to think about it. Elli was working, and he didn't know any of the other seed techs. "Yeah. Where do we go?"

The infirmary was located on the main floor. They had to walk through the dining area and enter an inconspicuous door near the back. That led them down a hallway that branched off into multiple private bathrooms. At the end, the door marked "MED BAY" was painted a bright yellow. There was no lock.

"It's very rare anyone comes here," Salomon explained as they waited in a small, well-lit lobby. There were no chairs, so they stood. An empty desk was before them, with a door to their right presumably leading to separate rooms. "If someone does come for an injury, it's generally something like what happened to Dr. Miller—weird accidents and such. Or occasionally, someone will come down with the cold or the flu. How diseases make their way into this place is beyond me."

"What's it like?" Jørn asked. "A normal day here, at the vault."

Salomon sighed and scratched his beard. Before, he'd maintained an upbeat personality, but here, he seemed tired.

"It's more exciting than it may seem," Salomon said. "Yes, we spend most of the day working, studying. Most everyone takes the weekends off. We have a theater where we screen movies daily, and there's a gym retrofitted for most exercise routines. I've been asking for a blasted piano for three years now, but they refuse to fly one out. They've sent some keyboards, so there's a bit of music.

"Each night, our community has dinner together. It can seem intimidating at first, but it's what keeps us all sane. And the constant rotation of people helps keep it fresh too. I'm one of the only few who've been here off and on consistently since it was built."

"Don't you get antsy?" Jørn asked. He knew it wasn't the most articulate question, but he'd thrown professionalism out the door the moment he'd heard AC/DC blasting through the vault's entrance.

"Definitely," Salomon said. "But I'd much rather spend all my time here than anywhere else. There's nothing left for me beyond these walls. The AUCV is my home now, and one day it will be my coffin."

Jørn allowed the moment to fall into quiet. He wanted to pry more into Salomon's life, ask him why he felt there was nothing for him outside of the vault, ask him how he managed to stay sane, or if he ever wished to leave. But he held his tongue, debating whether it was wise to ask those questions so soon. He waited too long to decide, and a nurse came around the corner. She wore purple scrubs, and her brown hair was tied into a bun. She plopped down behind the desk and flashed two lazy eyes at Salomon and Jørn.

"Yes, Salomon?" the nurse asked.

"Good afternoon, Con, you've been busy today. We're here to see Dr. Miller," he said, grinning.

"And this is . . .?" Con ignored Salomon's request.

"Jørn," Salomon said. "He's a mechanobiologist. Just got here today."

"Interesting. Nice to meet you, Jørn. I'm Con." She held out a hand. "How long will you be here?"

"A couple months." He shook her hand, thankful she was more friendly than Goran. "Nice to meet you too."

"How's Dr. Miller?" Salomon interrupted.

"He's a bit groggy."

"We don't mind."

Con pressed her lips together, then pointed in the direction she had come. "Back here."

"Thank you," Salomon said.

SEVEN:

The medical room had two beds divided by a curtain. One was empty.

In the other, Dr. Miller lay with his back propped up about thirty degrees. He was middle-aged, and the beginning of a peppered beard was on his stony face. His head was bandaged with white gauze—a sight so cliché and cartoonish that Jørn had to refrain from laughing. A tray next to him contained a half-eaten lunch. He appeared to be asleep.

"Dr. Miller!" Salomon said.

The scientist opened one eye, stared suspiciously at the two of them, and then promptly shut it again.

"Should I leave?" Jørn asked.

"Don't worry," Salomon said. "He's always like this. Really grumpy fellow."

"What could you possibly need?" Dr. Miller grunted. Salomon was right. He even *sounded* grumpy.

"Dr. Miller, this is Jørn. He's new. Mechanobiologist. Got here just today. Why don't you say hello?"

Dr. Miller nodded slightly but didn't say hello. "You came in here and woke me up to introduce me to a grad student?"

"No. We're checking up on you," Salomon said,

changing the topic. "Had no idea you injured yourself yesterday until a couple of the seed techs told me."

Dr. Miller didn't respond. He clearly wasn't one for words.

"Glad to see you're doing fine," Salomon said. He approached the bed, swung out two chairs tucked against the wall, sat down in one, and motioned at the other.

Hesitantly, Jørn took a seat. He wasn't sure how to feel about Dr. Miller, just like he wasn't sure how to feel about Goran. How many people in the vault were so wary of outsiders? Just these two? Jørn didn't think so. Though maybe it really was just what Salomon had said—they were so used to people coming and going, it wasn't worth their time to invest in a short-term relationship.

But at the same time, he couldn't blame them. This was a tight-knit community, one that was locked up inside of a mountain on the only unpopulated continent on Earth. Bonds would be strong, and strangers from the *outside world* would be unwelcome to some.

"What're you really here for?" Dr. Miller asked, his eyes still closed.

"Well," Salomon said, "something strange happened at the scene of your accident."

At this, Dr. Miller perked up. Both his eyes were open now. He even sat a little straighter in his bed. "What do you mean?"

"Before I tell you," Salomon said, "I want you to tell me exactly what happened."

Dr. Miller chewed on his lip. He seemed unsure, which was the only emotion aside from annoyance that Jørn had seen the man show.

"I can't explain it," he said. He looked away from them, down at his hands, which were folded in his lap. "I went to The Box to retrieve some seeds—nothing out of the ordinary. When I walked through the door, I felt a dozen zaps up and down my body, like a shock from static electricity."

Dr. Miller paused.

"Then?" Salomon urged.

"Then I—I felt like I was floating. It was brief, and I must admit it could have been my imagination. It *must have been* my imagination."

"Your head wound," Jørn said, "how did that happen?"

"We can chalk up the sensation of floating to a lapse in my logic, to external environmental pressures that only made me *feel* like I was floating," Dr. Miller said. "But I cannot rationally explain what happened next.

"I was thrown into the metal shelving. No, I didn't trip, I didn't stumble, I didn't accidentally bump my head—I was *violently* thrown into the shelves. The doc told me my head looks like someone took the back end of a hammer to my skull. That doesn't happen from a mere misstep. Something threw me against those shelves. I woke up here. Doc stitched my head up, said she was surprised I didn't suffer a concussion."

Jørn rubbed his hands together, unsure what to think about the situation. Even Salomon seemed hesitant to respond. He cradled his chin in his thumb and forefinger, staring at Dr. Miller's bandage.

"Now tell me what strange thing happened at the scene of my accident," Dr. Miller said, pointing a fat finger at Salomon.

"Much like the story you told me," Salomon said, "I don't know what to make of what we found in The Box." He glanced behind him. Someone had just rushed past the door's window, a blur of dark hair.

"The blood from your wound froze into a puddle," Salomon explained. "A plant was growing in it."

The only thing that broke the silence in the room was the sound of another person running past the door. Jørn looked back again. What was going on? Was there an emergency?

"What do you mean a plant was growing in it?" Dr. Miller asked.

"Straight out of it," Salomon said. "Like your blood mixed with snow was no different from the Earth's soil. It was getting nutrients from somewhere. We're running tests on it now."

"What do you think it means?" Dr. Miller asked. He relaxed into his bed again, half shutting his eyes.

"We have no idea," Salomon said. "Your recollection of the events surrounding your injury only adds further mystery to the situation. But we'll have answers soon; we always do. Besides, Jørn here is our first mechanobiologist. And he already has formed a theory about how this plant is living off blood. If anyone can figure out exactly what happened to cause a plant to grow in blood, it'll be him."

Dr. Miller sighed. "Pfft. Mechanobiologists."

Salomon opened his mouth, but Jørn held out a hand. "It's fine," he said. "I get that a lot. People fear what they don't understand."

Dr. Miller shot Jørn a nasty look, but he didn't acknowledge it.

"We'll come back soon with answers," Salomon said as he stood from his chair. "Get feeling better, Dr. Miller."

"It was nice to meet you," Jørn said.

When he turned to leave, he saw yet another person rush past the door. "Salomon, I think something's happening."

"I'm sure they're just running a drill or something," Salomon said.

The door to their room opened at once, and the nurse from the front desk poked her head in. "Salomon," she said, "one of the seed techs had an accident in The Box. It's pretty serious."

He looked back at Jørn, who looked back at Dr. Miller, who stared at them both with squinted eyes. "How much do you wanna bet the same thing that happened to me just happened to that seed tech?"

Salomon frowned. "I desperately hope not."

EIGHT:

The seed tech who was injured turned out to be Goran. Even delirious, he still scowled. Jørn wondered if Goran just didn't like him or if his lousy mood was perpetual.

"Well," Salomon said, running a hand through his beard as he stepped up next to Goran's bed, "how are you feeling?"

"Crappy," Goran said.

The nurse and the doctor had finished wrapping his head moments ago and had left the room to check on Dr. Miller. Pumped full of medicine and ensured that his injury wasn't life-threatening, Goran looked displeased with the entire scenario.

"Do you want to tell me what happened?" Salomon asked.

Goran shook his head, but winced at the movement. "You won't believe me."

"Funny you should say that," Salomon replied, sitting on the edge of the bed. "Dr. Miller told us the same thing. And we believed him, didn't we, Jørn?"

Jørn cleared his throat. "Y-yes," he said.

Goran considered their words for a moment, raising his hand to lightly touch the gauze wrapping his head.

"I'll tell you," he said, looking at Salomon. "But I don't want him here." He shot a pointed look at Jørn.

Salomon looked back at Jørn apologetically and mouthed something that could have been "we'll talk later," though it was hard to tell through his facial hair.

"All right," he said. "I'm going."

—

Roughly an hour later, Jørn stepped under the spewing hot water of a private shower. He'd spent some of that hour wandering the vault, getting familiar with the layout. Then he'd asked a random seed tech where the berthing quarters were, and the seed tech had directed him to an area past the labs.

He'd found his room easy enough—a plaque with his name was stuck to the door. And Salomon had been right—someone had brought his bag to his room. He'd spent a few minutes lying down, processing the day's events, trying to wrap his head around a plant that grew in blood and, supposedly, two people who were attacked by an invisible force. Then, when he'd had enough of thinking, he'd gone to the showers, which were just down the hall from the bedrooms. For a moment, he'd feared they were communal—he didn't want to spend two months sharing a shower with a bunch of strangers—but was happy to find that the ten showers were divided into stalls with thick walls and doors that stayed flush with the ground and ceiling. He imagined it was the most privacy one could get in the vault.

It felt good to be alone and to warm up. He still felt cold from disembarking the helicopter, and the water helped change that.

What am I doing here? The thought hit him with such suddenness that he nearly slipped.

He was excited to be here at the legendary AUCV; he

was eager to get into his studies and meet the other scientists. But a huge part of him felt unprepared and unqualified. And while the idea of being locked inside of a mountain hadn't seemed so bad at first, now that he was here, it was beginning to feel claustrophobic.

He'd loved biology, specifically plant biology, since he was a kid. His parents had encouraged this passion by enrolling him in various clubs and pushing him academically. And while he'd struggled in certain areas of school—art, fitness, history—he'd soared in the sciences, even in English, since so much of science was based around writing. In his senior year of high school, he'd already been offered enrollment at three major universities.

Then the announcement had come: A few significant countries in the world would combine their efforts to build a lab in the mountains of Antarctica. There, the "seeds of the world" would be stored, studied, and experimented upon. Its purpose was mainly to do research in a neutral location, but it was designed to withstand "cataclysmic levels of destruction." The announcement had, of course, caused an uproar of conspiracy theories. Many people thought the government was hinting they were aware of something the public wasn't, something huge like a world war, an alien invasion, or an approaching asteroid. Most people realized what it really was: a way for the government to spend more money.

Nevertheless, when it was announced, Jørn immediately desired to work there. He'd already been interested in mechanobiology, and the idea of being a leading expert in that field while also working in the AUCV was thrilling.

He'd worked tirelessly for years to be here, so why was he feeling so uncertain?

He turned the shower off, deciding his thoughts

would bring him no comfort and that it was better to begin working.

The bathroom was empty. Jørn dried off, cursing when he realized he'd left his clean clothes in his bedroom. He wrapped the towel around his waist and departed.

When he stepped out of the bathroom, he froze.

Elli was standing at the door leading to her bedroom, which just so happened to be across the hall from Jørn's. She, too, was wrapped only in a towel. Her blonde hair was wet and clung to her cheeks and her neck.

It was the first time Jørn had ever seen her without makeup. Elli was the kind of girl who always looked like she'd spent a considerable amount of time getting ready. And while he'd always thought she was beautiful, he felt like he was looking at a far more perfect version of her.

He stammered, and she glanced at him. Her lips twisted into a devious smile.

"Don't look so embarrassed, Jørn," she said. "I'm not completely naked."

Jørn's face burned hotter. He wanted to look away, but he couldn't. The harsh lighting bounced off her bare shoulders, making her glow in an ethereal way.

Elli opened her door, but kept her eyes on him. "Let me put some clothes on, and then we can get some dinner together."

She winked at him.

His heart nearly exploded in his chest.

She stepped inside and shut her door.

NINE:

The cafeteria was brimming with people. Jørn had met so few of them that he'd started thinking the vault didn't have that many employees. But there were at least fifty people here.

Jørn and Elli fell into line behind the serving counter. He had yet to speak to her, and she hadn't acknowledged their run-in outside of the showers. However, he was surprised to see that she had opted for no makeup.

"Do you wanna hear a joke?" Jørn asked. He needed the nervous, awkward tension between them to disappear.

"If it's another one of your puns, then no."

"Did you know mountains aren't *just* funny?"

Elli eyed him suspiciously. "What do you mean?"

Jørn pressed his fist to his mouth. "They're *hill areas*."

"Jørn," she said, her voice much lower than usual, "go get help."

He chuckled, and he caught a slight smile on her face before she rubbed it away.

The line moved slowly but steadily. People wearing all types of clothing, from full parkas to rolled-down jumpsuits that exposed wifebeaters underneath, carried trays of food to nearby tables, joining their groups of friends.

Eventually, Elli and Jørn reached the serving counter.

A man wearing a black apron stood before an array of vegetables, fruits, stew, and green Jell-O. He wore a paper chef's hat and had a huge smile that revealed crooked teeth.

When they approached the counter, his smile seemed to widen.

"You two must be new," he said in a thick accent Jørn couldn't identify. "What was your names, then?"

"I'm Elli," she said, smiling. "This is Jørn."

"Elli. Jørn." The man spoke their names as if they tasted strange. "Nice to meet you both."

"What's your name?" Elli asked.

"My name be Braddock," he said. "Now, what is it you both like?" He waved his hand over the food.

Elli picked mostly fruit and then opted for a boxed salad Jørn had failed to notice. He went with the fruit as well, but decided on the stew. The shower had not entirely cured his desire for total warmth. His stomach needed heating up.

Jørn and Elli managed to find a table in the corner of the cafeteria. A few people waved to them, but nobody moved to introduce themselves.

"How was studying the blood plant?" Jørn asked once they'd sat down.

"Good," Elli said. "It's a plant quite literally growing out of blood. So honestly, it's fascinating."

"Well, did you find anything?" Jørn asked. He took a sip of the stew. It scalded his lips, but the taste was strong. If this was how the rest of the food was, then he couldn't complain. He'd had far, far worse on research trips before.

"Asta, the girl who did most of the work, confirmed the plant is feeding off the blood. She found blood in the veins, as well as in the microvessels of the sprout."

"Any theories on how that works?"

"Not yet," Elli said, taking a bite from her salad. "Obviously, we assume the plant is carnivorous, but we know bloodroot isn't. It must be a modified version of bloodroot."

"Okay," Jørn said. "Turn off your scientist brain for a moment. Based on your gut, what do you think it is?"

Elli sighed, and he continued shoving spoonfuls of stew into his mouth.

"Obviously, I don't know *anything*," she said. "However, while I was in the lab, I overheard something about a security breach a few years ago. Apparently, one of the countries whose scientists aren't invited to study here sent them a contaminated batch of seeds. It made one of the techs extremely ill, so much so that he was flown out of here. It could be something like that—it's the only thing that makes sense, really. Plants don't grow in just blood."

"That guess isn't as crazy as it sounds," Jørn said. "Salomon and I talked to Dr. Miller."

"And what did he say?"

Jørn repeated what Dr. Miller had told them. When he was done, he expected some sort of reaction from Elli, confusion or excitement. Instead, she stared at him blankly.

"He doesn't believe in mechanobiology?" she asked.

"That's what you got from the story?"

"He made a snide comment about mechanobiology."

"Well, yes, but—"

"I can't believe he has the audacity to make fun of your profession when he just got beaten up by some invisible seed monster."

Jørn laughed. It was the first genuine laugh he'd had in days.

"It's not a big deal," he said, still smiling. "There are

plenty of scientists who don't see the merit in a mecha-nobiologist. Anyway, I guess the same thing happened to Goran, that ornery seed tech, right after. We went to see him, but he didn't want me there."

"What do you mean the same thing happened?"

"He had a head wound too," Jørn explained. "Happened in The Box as well. Obviously, something's going on in there. I wouldn't be surprised if it's some sort of infected seed that's messing with people's brains."

"We were in there," Elli said, lowering her fork away from her mouth.

Jørn widened his eyes. "It's probably best if we spend absolutely no time alone, especially in The Box."

"The buddy system," she said.

"Exactly. Do you wanna be my buddy?"

Elli blushed. It passed quicker than it came, but Jørn had caught it. It gave him a strange, excited feeling.

Before she could answer, heavy footsteps rang through the dining hall. Jørn looked over to see Salomon jogging toward one of the tables. He carried a small glass vial, and he seemed frazzled.

He stopped at the table. Jørn recognized one of the people sitting there as Asta. They appeared to argue for a moment, until eventually Salomon looked up, found Jørn and Elli, and waved them over.

"What do you think he wants?" she asked.

"No idea." Jørn stood up as a surge of courage ran through him. He didn't know where it came from or why, but in that split second of pure confidence, he grabbed Elli's hand and led her to Salomon.

She didn't pull away.

TEN:

Everyone at the table leaned in, staring at a small vial Salomon had placed there for them all to see. When Jørn and Elli arrived, they had to squeeze their way through the circle of onlookers to get a proper view.

At first, Jørn thought the vial was filled with nothing more than blood, but upon closer inspection, he realized it also contained a few seeds—one of them already sprouting.

"Where did you get this?" Elli asked.

Salomon swallowed hard. He looked nervous, as if he didn't want to answer the question, but the stares of everyone in the cafeteria must have been successful at pressuring him.

"Con, the nurse, pulled it out of Goran's wound."

The cafeteria fell silent.

"Out of his *wound*?" Asta asked.

Salomon nodded. "Right when he arrived, they cleaned him up and pulled this out of his head. Didn't tell him, of course. The last thing a distressed patient needs to hear is that their head is sprouting plants."

Jørn cleared his throat. "Is it a seed that fell into his wound after he was injured?"

"I don't think so," Salomon said. "The nurse had to

pry it out of him. Unless it grew at an inexplicable rate, it must have been growing inside him before that."

"It could be a modified seed," Asta said.

Jørn glanced around. Everyone had left their table, now peering over pairs and pairs of shoulders to see and hear what was going on.

"Maybe," Salomon said. "But Goran usually deals with shipment-only seeds."

"What does that mean?" Elli asked. Jørn's hand was still wrapped around hers. What this meant, he had no idea. But he liked being this close to her.

"Shipment-only seeds," Asta explained, "refers to the seeds sent to us that are meant only for storage."

"He was in the lab today," Kennet said. The seed tech was forcing his way through the crowd, the camera still around his neck.

"I'm not saying it's impossible he somehow got . . . *infected* by a seed we mutated," Salomon said. "I just don't think it's likely."

"It would have to be carnivorous, right?" Asta picked up the vial and held it closer to her face. Other people leaned in closer to see.

"Maybe," Salomon said.

"There's only one way to find out," Asta said. Without warning, she stood swiftly from her seat, closed her hand around the vial, and left in the direction of the lab.

Everybody followed.

—

Jørn and Elli sat hand-in-hand a table away from Asta. She wore goggles and gloves and had an array of equipment laid out before her. It was the first time Jørn noticed a Nepalese bracelet hanging from her wrist. She was doing preliminary work, mainly taking notes and allowing Kennet to photograph the subject. As she worked, everyone else waited patiently, talking amongst themselves. It was strange to see an entire lab full of people dressed in casual clothing. It reminded Jørn of his high school years.

"Is there anything in mechanobiology that can help us understand what's going on?" Salomon asked. He sat next to Jørn, but kept his eyes trained on Asta.

"It's still considered an emerging field," Jørn said. "But the entire idea behind mechanobiology is that the slightest difference in environmental factors can change the entire structure of plants, even down to their smallest cells."

"Would a controlled environment like ours be able to change a cell's system so drastically that it begins to grow from blood?"

"I don't know," Jørn said. "This is a vastly different environment than almost any other on Earth. I mean, the number of spores in the air alone is concerning, let alone the varying temperatures, millions of different seeds, and the close-quarters environment. I wouldn't be surprised if the environment contributed to the strange behavior of this plant, but I doubt it was the entire cause."

Elli pulled her hand away from Jørn's, and before he could turn to her, she'd hopped off her seat and wandered close to Asta.

"After finding the plant in Goran's head, the nurse rechecked Dr. Miller's wound. Luckily, they found nothing," Saloman said.

"And Goran claimed the same thing happened to him that happened to Dr. Miller?" Jørn asked.

"Beat by beat."

"Then obviously—" Jørn fell silent when Asta reached

for the microscope and swung it out in front of her. She opened the lid of the vial and the plant, poured a bit onto a slide, and inserted it in the microscope.

A giant screen lit up above all their heads on the far wall. It was a perfect view of what Asta saw through the microscope. When she adjusted its focus, the screen changed focus too.

They were staring at what looked like a mottled mess, but Asta quickly adjusted the microscope, and soon it became clear what they were looking at: the plant's stem. Everyone in the lab immediately broke out in whispers. Jørn stayed quiet. They all understood what they were seeing.

The stem was filled with red blood cells.

Asta wrote down a few things on her notepad and moved the microscope's lens until it hovered over one of the tiny leaves. She zoomed in, and everyone waited patiently for her to focus the view.

The leaf, too, was running rampant with red blood cells. They coursed through the plant's veins in place of chlorophyll.

"I don't think the plant is surviving off photosynthesis," Asta said, turning to face Salomon.

For once, the gray-bearded scientist was out of words.

"I think it's using human blood to live."

At Asta's words, the lab went into a frenzy. Everyone began shouting excitedly, rushing to and fro between the tables. Kennet snapped pictures of the entire event. The group of scientists clamored over each other, aiming for a better view of what lay underneath the microscope.

"We are part of something big here," Salomon said. "For better or for worse, I think we're witnessing something extraordinary."

Jørn swallowed. "You're right about the lack of photosynthesis here. There are many gases found in blood, and I'm thinking here that because carbon dioxide is a waste product of cellular respiration, the plant is harnessing it somehow, so it doesn't need photosynthesis. Heck, carbon dioxide exists in three forms: dissolved in plasma, bound to hemoglobin, and as bicarbonate ions. So it can have access to this gas from many constituents of blood."

The strange, uncomfortable feeling in his gut had returned. This plant lived off blood pumping through its veins.

ELEVEN:

Within a couple of hours, the excitement had settled down. Roughly half the scientists had left the lab, either to finish their dinner or retire to bed. Jørn had remained alone with Elli, Asta, Kennet, Salomon, and several other nameless scientists.

Jørn stayed in his seat, watching from a distance. Asta's table was already crowded enough, and he doubted he could add anything helpful to the conversation until they had more data.

It was halfway through the second hour since Asta's discovery that Salomon left the lab and reappeared with a stack of papers.

He dropped them on Jørn's table with a sigh. "I'm really sorry I have to ask this of you," he said. "But I set aside all this paperwork for you before you even arrived, and the mainland is waiting on your analysis."

"Busywork?" Jørn asked.

Salomon sighed again. "Unfortunately, our grants and our funding rely on busywork."

Jørn laughed, looped his arm around the stack of papers, and slid them closer to him. "It's my favorite!"

"Thanks," Salomon said. "I'm sure we'll have something more concrete from the blood plant tomorrow. That way, you'll be able to study something exciting."

Jørn nodded and turned to the papers, and Salomon returned to Asta's table.

The stack of papers wasn't too daunting to him—he'd dealt with far bigger. And it wasn't nearly as boring as Salomon had led him to believe. Maybe the papers would be boring to anyone outside of mechanobiology, but Jørn found them fascinating. It was mainly a report of over four dozen plants and how they had reacted differently to other environments. At one point, Jørn had to seek out a pen. He had thoughts on many of the studies and needed some way to make notes.

Without a doubt, plants were acting differently than they would in the wild. The AUCV was a strange, one-of-a-kind environment, so the data he had was also one of a kind.

Grown entirely under artificial sunlight and on a continent where nothing was supposed to grow, it was no surprise to find that the data was slightly off from what he'd seen before. While he'd yet to find any groundbreaking information in the papers, it was just further proof that mechanobiology was a legitimate field.

"Salomon has you doing busywork, huh?"

Jørn looked up. A woman stood next to his table. She was much shorter than Elli. Her red hair fell to her shoulders, and she had brown eyes and thin, sharp lips. Her name tag read "Lovise."

"I guess." Jørn smiled.

Lovise laughed, then pulled out a seat next to him. When she sat down, a waft of tropical-scented perfume swept past him.

"I'm Lovise," she said, holding out a hand with painted fingernails.

"Jørn," he said, shaking her hand.

"You must be new here?" The question seemed to drip from her mouth.

"Arrived earlier today."

"Ah, yes. I remember my first day."

Jørn looked back to his papers. Why was he so *awkward*? Why couldn't he just look her in the eyes and have a steady conversation with her?

"How long have you been here?" he asked.

"Three months. I leave on the next ride out of here." She placed her elbows on the table and rested her head in her hands. "I can't wait."

"You don't like it here?" Jørn asked. He forced himself to shift his body toward her.

"I *do* like it here, but being so cut off from the world is . . . hard. No friends, no family, no current movies, no restaurants. Just the vault and the same scientists, same sights, same smells, same sounds every day."

Jørn smiled. "It is kind of weird that some people don't mind spending more than a few months here. I'm excited to be here and all, but it's not like I'd particularly want to stay a very long time."

"Yes!" Lovise shouted. "Like Salomon—the man has been here forever and has no plan to leave anytime soon. I can't believe it."

"Unbe*leaf*able," Jørn said, biting his lip.

Lovise looked at him, eyes narrowed, and for a moment, Jørn thought she'd give him the same reaction Elli always did. But then she smiled.

"That was pretty good, pun boy."

"You didn't hate it?"

"I think you could do better," she teased, "but no, I didn't hate it."

"Well," Salomon said, speaking at a volume so loud he interrupted every single private conversation in the lab.

"I'm going to bed." He sauntered away from the table, a handful of people following him. Asta and Elli were still focused solely on their work.

"Are you staying up a while longer?" Lovise asked. Did she look slightly hopeful, or was it just Jørn's imagination? "I could stay with you."

"I don't want to admit it," he said, "but I'm exhausted."

"I figured as much."

"But I'll see you tomorrow?" Jørn asked, his blood running cool.

She nodded, smiling, a slight pink appearing on her cheeks.

"Good," he said.

Lovise left the table, turning back only to wave at him. Once she was gone, Jørn picked up his papers and departed the lab.

TWELVE:

The next morning, Jørn awoke before his seven a.m. alarm. He lay in bed for a few minutes, thinking about the insane events of the day before, but eventually got to his feet and headed for the showers.

Half an hour later, once he was ready for the day, he followed a clump of scientists to the cafeteria. It was in more of a full swing than dinner the night before. People were excitable, chatty, and most of all, curious. The discovery of the blood-hungry plant the previous night seemed to have had a widespread social effect.

Jørn searched for Elli or Lovise and, unable to find either, settled into the back of the line. He tuned everyone out as he tried to get a better view of what they were serving for breakfast. Steam from the food line finally caught his nose. Sausage, hot maple syrup, and eggs were on the menu today. He swallowed. He was starving. He hoped it was filling.

"Hi, you."

Jørn startled.

"A bit jumpy, you are," Lovise said. She was wearing her white lab coat—something he had yet to find—and she'd tied her red hair up into a messy bun.

"Sorry," he said.

"Don't apologize, pun boy. I'm the one who scared you." She elbowed him playfully.

They chatted as they moved through the crawling line. Jørn learned she was from Michigan and that she'd graduated high school a year early and then gone to Connecticut to attend Yale on a full-ride scholarship. Unlike most biologists Jørn knew, she had a wide-ranging taste and opinion of pop culture, everything from rock bands to slow-burn thriller movies to the latest social media influencer drama.

By the time they'd gathered their breakfast trays—waffles stuffed with fruit, eggs, bacon, and sausage—and found a table, Jørn felt he knew Lovise better than he knew Elli.

The thought struck him as odd. Conversation had never been this easy, this effervescent, with Elli. Was this how a girl acted when she was interested? Had he been fooling himself this whole time?

"So," Lovise said, "do you watch horror movies?"

"I've seen the classics," Jørn admitted, tearing into his waffle, "but not much of the newer stuff."

"Carpenter or Craven?" she asked as she nibbled at her food.

"Probably Craven," Jørn said. "I think both are tremendous, but Craven has *Scream* while Carpenter has *Halloween*, and *Scream* just has such a better track record than *Halloween*."

"But Carpenter didn't have a whole lot of say in the sequels to *Halloween*," Lovise said, "whereas Craven is responsible for *Scream 3*."

"*Scream 3* gets hated on too much. The first half isn't any good, I'll give you that, but the second half is fun. It's at least half of a good movie."

"Whatever you say. I'm a Carpenter girl through and through."

Out of the corner of his eye, Jørn saw Salomon approaching their table. He held a giant stack of manila envelopes, and he slapped two down next to their trays.

"These are the results from last night. Asta ended up dissecting the plants. I want everybody on this right now."

Jørn looked around and saw others already scanning through packets. Then he spotted Elli. She was still in line for breakfast, her back to him.

"I sent these to the mainland," Salomon said. "There are probably hundreds of scientists over there studying the same data we are. We'll have an explanation soon enough . . . I hope."

A commotion near the entrance drew everyone's attention. A group of people—mostly men—were gathered around someone, moving toward an empty table near the corner.

"Looks like Goran's out of the infirmary," Salomon said.

Sure enough, when the group reached the table and sat down, Goran was revealed. His head was still bandaged, but he looked to be in better spirits.

"I better go see how he's doing," Salomon said.

Jørn leaned in close to Lovise. "Is Goran a . . . grumpy person?"

She nodded, her mouth full of waffles.

"Rough around the *hedges*?" Jørn asked.

Lovise coughed as she tried to swallow while holding in laughter, and Jørn could tell she got his joke.

"I'm gonna go check on him too," he said. "Will you watch my food?"

Lovise nodded, gave him a thumbs-up, and continued to chew.

The table was filled with many seed techs Jørn didn't know except for Goran and Kennet. They were acting as men always did: idiotically excited about a serious injury. Pointing at Goran's head bandage. One seed tech lifted the edge, trying to sneak a peek at the wound, but was slapped down by another seed tech. Goran leaned away before saying something to the man who tried to look at his head.

Jørn sidled up next to Salomon.

"Goran," Salomon said, "how are you feeling?"

Goran leaned back in his chair, a strip of bacon pinched between his fingers, and shot him a genuine smile. "I'm doing good, Salomon. Thanks for asking. Feel much better than I did yesterday."

"And the nurse inspected your wound again?"

"Just before I came here. Says it's healing remarkably fast."

"I'm glad to hear it," Salomon said. "Turns out that plant inside your head was living off your blood. Who knows how bad it could have gotten if we hadn't caught it when we did?"

"That's what these guys were telling me. Is that the data?" Goran pointed at the files Salomon held.

"Yes," he said, depositing a stack on the table. The seed techs all took one and began perusing its contents.

"It doesn't need sunlight, then?" Goran asked.

"Apparently not," Salomon replied. "Like I said, your blood was acting as its source of nutrients, and somehow, it was able to complete photosynthesis just off of your heme. It may have kept growing if we hadn't pulled it out."

"Cool." Goran absentmindedly reached up and touched his bandage.

"You think you can work today?" Salomon asked.

"Absolutely," he replied. "Kincaid said I should be able to."

"All right, let's get to it," Salomon said.

Jørn had just returned back to his table and finished his first bite when Goran and Kennet got up to go to the lab. He popped a piece of sausage in his mouth as the guilt set in. With hunger gone, he felt compelled to follow the seed techs to the lab and get to work as well. While he walked to dump his plate, he sliced a syrup-soaked piece of pancake and shoved it into his mouth.

Elli passed with a plate full of food. "Morning, what are you doing? Did you eat already?" she asked.

"Yeah. I'm going to go help Goran and Kennet for the morning."

"Goran's okay?"

"Totally. Kincaid cleared him, and I think they're going to study the blood plant, so I'd like to be there. Come join us after you eat, okay?"

"Okay," Elli replied.

Jørn strolled out of the cafeteria, turning back to see her sitting with Lovise.

THIRTEEN:

Asta had placed blood agar gel into petri dishes and had them all lined up on a lab table. She watched them intently.

"Impressive," Jørn said. "Where did you get all the blood from?"

Asta looked down and pulled up her lab coat sleeves to reveal plump gauze pads folded under bandages taped to the crook of her arms.

Jørn smiled. He walked up to the lab bench, hesitated, then approached slowly, leaning in. "How long did it take to grow these?"

"Thirteen hours," Asta responded.

"They're samples from the plant that sprouted from my head," Goran said.

Kennet took pictures of all the spindly green sprouts in every petri dish from all different angles.

"Lights were illuminated six minutes ago," Asta said. "They grew in the dark."

Jørn knew of plants that grew in the dark, but that was in a pot with soil and water. Not blood agar. Most were thin, twisting tendrils reaching above the lip of the petri dish. Not a fascinating feat since the glassware was only an inch in height and they sat next to another at the end of the row that had sprouted tiny vines with dime-size leaves. Jørn quickly moved to that one to examine it.

"That's Dr. Miller's sample. Its twenty-four hours old," Asta said.

Jørn took a small glass rod and lifted one of the little vines to inspect underneath. It seemed more red, as if blood had pooled there. Goran approached and Jørn slid over for him to take a look as well. He removed the glass rod, but to their surprise, the vine didn't fall back to the table. It seemed to float, to reach and stretch . . . toward Goran's bandage.

"Look at this, Asta," Jørn said.

She joined them by the bigger plant. As Goran shifted, so did the vine, until other vines from Dr. Miller's sample lifted off the table and extended toward him. Almost as if he were some sort of plant magnet.

"That is odd," Asta said, and then without warning grabbed the back of Goran's neck and led him to every one of the petri dishes that showed signs of plant life. All the little green sprouts stretched, tremoring toward Goran. They seemed so helpless, but wanted so badly to be close to him.

"Let me get that on video," Kennet said. He pushed a couple of buttons on the screen of his camera, held it up, and said, "Action!"

Asta pushed Goran's head toward one of the sprouts. It stretched as far as it could. Jørn almost thought it looked cute. Such a small, innocent thing reaching to be held closer to him.

Without warning, Goran stood up straight, arching his back. "I don't like that!"

"I'm sorry," Asta said. "I got carried away."

"Seems sorry should be nice not," Goran said.

Jørn raised an eyebrow and looked at the seed tech.

Goran pointed at the petri dishes. "Like not but nuts strange fascinating."

Jørn shot Asta a look. She shrugged. "Are you feeling okay, Goran?" she asked.

Kennet stopped filming and stared.

Jørn grabbed Goran's hand and put his index and middle fingers on the soft inside of his wrist to take a quick pulse.

"No yes, but the thing green me," Goran said, as if nothing was wrong.

"I'm going to go get Dr. Kincaid," Jørn said. He rushed out of the room.

Kincaid returned with Jørn in tow. The vault's doctor put his arm around Goran. "Let's go to my office for a minute and talk."

"Smacks happy doc finally," Goran said, smiling, and he let Dr. Kincaid lead him out of the lab and down the hall.

FOURTEEN:

That night Jørn sat alone in the cafeteria. He hadn't seen Elli all day. In fact, he hadn't seen Salomon the rest of the day either.

Hot meatloaf with tangy barbeque sauce sat untouched while he was lost in his thoughts. Could the plant have caused Goran's speech symptoms? Why were the seedlings attracted to him? Fortunately, that afternoon Jørn had received word that Goran was fine, and it wasn't a stroke. The predominant theory was it had something to do with the medication Dr. Kincaid had had him on. A weird side-effect reaction.

He slid a chart in a manila folder from under his dinner tray. Small rust-colored droplets of blood splatter stained the front.

Asta's blood, he thought.

The first page in the chart had Goran's results. He thought it odd that anyone could have access to Dr. Kincaid's notes about Goran's checkups. He supposed they were all scientists, so it wasn't a big issue.

Nothing out of the ordinary. Jørn's eyes fell to the list of medications Goran was taking after the fall, which didn't give any more clues as to why he was speaking so weird. Maybe there was a toxin in the seeds that were extracted from his wound? Jørn flipped to the next page and the next while he absentmindedly stirred his mashed potatoes with a fork.

The plant was a Dominico-Hartón plantain from Colombia. A False Horn cultivar: genus Musa. Jørn was still caught up in thought when Elli came up to him. Startled, he flicked mashed potatoes all over the cafeteria table.

"What do you have there?" she asked.

Jørn grabbed a napkin and wiped up the glob of potato. "Meatloaf and mashed—"

"No, not your dinner, ha ha."

"Oh, the findings and hypothesis of what's going on with Goran and in Asta's lab."

"Interesting. Did they find out anything?"

"There are definitely some ideas, but they don't have a *fern* grasp on what happened to Goran." Jørn smiled.

This time Elli smiled back as well. He had either worn her down with his brilliant plant puns and she was giving him sympathy, or she had finally started to see the stupid humor in them. Either way, Jørn was glad she sat next to him.

"The plant was a plantain," he said. "Isn't that crazy? A plantain, Elli. What's a plantain doing surviving off someone's blood? I mean, there's carnivorous plant species, but I've never heard of a blood-sucking plantain before, have you?"

"Not to my knowledge." She blinked slowly, then turned back to her food and started to eat. This cue gave Jørn license to dig in also. The individual papers he read were attached with two round paper fasteners at the top, so he let them settle back into the folder before closing it and turning to his supper.

He'd neglected his food long enough that the meatloaf

was a cube of lukewarm seasoned meat and the gravy had congealed in puddles around the mashed potatoes.

"I've gotta be honest with you, Elli," Jørn said. "I'm so exhausted. Today has been crazy. Don't you think?"

"It's definitely not the introduction I was expecting to have when we got here. I mean, I knew that AUCV had a lot of eccentric minds, and I was interested in meeting everyone, but with this blood plant and everyone focused on Goran and such, I feel like it's going to be hard to conduct our research outside the scope of this blood plantain thing."

"That's true. I totally see your point."

"Don't get me wrong, I think the focus should be on Goran at this point. He's injured, and we all need to get to the bottom of it so that he can get better."

"Maybe it'll make him less of a grump," Lovise interrupted, dropping her tray next to Elli. "Mind if I join you guys?"

"Go for it," Elli replied.

Jørn simply smiled. He took a heaping bite of his meatloaf. The savory-sweet flavor put his salivary glands in overload. Hunger exploded to the surface, and he ate—lukewarm or not. He hadn't realized how hungry he really was until now. Elli cut a piece of her own meatloaf and speared it with her fork. She scooped a generous dollop of mashed potato onto the same fork and took a bite. Lovise ate as if she were in a timed event, finishing way before them.

When they had eaten enough, Jørn said, "Here, let me empty your trays for you guys."

"Ah, thank you, Jørn," Elli said. "You're always taking care of me."

"Funny and chivalrous, pun boy?" Lovise winked.

"You think he's funny?" Elli frowned.

"Yeah, anyone can be crude for a laugh," Lovise said. "But not everyone can be clever."

Jørn's face reddened as he stacked their trays on top of his dirty dishes and skillfully carried them to the trash can. If Elli had said that to him two days ago, he would have been crushed. He realized just how inexperienced he was in the dating world. Elli was gorgeous and he liked being around her, but it wasn't a romantic connection. Not like he had with Lovise.

Someone came in to get dinner, and the cold air from the hallway gave him a chill. With the trays empty and stacked for the crew on duty to do dishes, he turned back to Elli and Lovise. Except Elli had left the table in favor of another scientist's company. He studied her body language. She tousled her hair and laughed loudly at something he said, then playfully slapped his shoulder. Jørn shook his head. He should have realized he'd been friend-zoned months ago.

"All right," he said. "All done."

"Thank you so much for doing that," Lovise said. "You're a *plantastic* guy."

Jørn's eyes widened. Did he hear what he thought he heard? His mouth moved, but nothing came out.

Lovise beamed, showing her beautiful white teeth. "Yeah, yeah, I know. I used a plant pun, and it didn't work well."

"It, it . . ." Jørn started. He shook his head. "No, no . . . I mean." He looked down at his permafrost-covered boots and whispered to himself, "Get it together, man."

He looked up at Lovise. She blinked slowly and cocked her head.

"I just can't believe you used a pun, Lovise." Jørn stepped toward her and awkwardly put his hand on her shoulder. She looked at his hand and back to him. "It truly was perfect."

"All right, all right." Lovise stood. "Don't get all excited. That'll be the first and last time for sure. Probably."

Jørn stepped back as she moved away from the table. "There's a special place in my heart for a good plant pun. And that was a fantastic one!"

"I know!" Lovise smiled again. "Don't make me regret saying it."

"I won't," Jørn said. "May I walk you to the women's berth?"

"My room?" she asked.

"Yes, your room."

"You're being all weird now. Berth?"

"Well, that's what they call it."

"I know, but it just sounds so weird. Plus, the women's berth is right across the hall from the men's berth."

"True. Okay. It would be *plantastic* if you'd allow me to walk you to your room." Jørn put one hand over his navel and one hand behind the small of his back and bowed slightly like a proper English butler would do.

She pushed him on the shoulder, and Jørn almost toppled over. He wasn't known for his athleticism or balance. "I suppose. Sure," she said.

The flirtatious banter continued as the two of them walked to the berthing wing in the frozen bowels of the AUCV. Jørn finally decided that he was going to really like it here.

FIFTEEN:

Jørn's room was shared by a scruffy-bearded seed tech named Rutger. He always wore his green expedition parka no matter the activity, including sleeping. The red and blue patch over the left breast had been seared at one point, making the thread clump up into hard nylon nodules. Jørn couldn't wait to get to know him better so he could feel comfortable enough to ask what had happened.

Rutger sat on the end of his bed and removed his boots and thick wool socks. Jørn thought it was weird that he would eat, sleep, and work with the parka on, but then sleep barefoot. He stretched his long, bony toes before lying back on his bed, fully clothed except for socks and boots, of course.

"How are you doing?" Jørn asked.

Rutger raised an eyebrow. "Spectacular, terrific, fantastic, joyous, tranquil, stupendous, wonderful."

"Okay." Jørn nodded slowly.

"How are *you* doing?" Rutger bounced back the question.

Jørn rubbed the back of his neck. "I'm good. Honestly, a little stressed. I've got to do a bunch of research, but I feel like I'm not going to have enough time to get—"

Rutger held his hand up. "I'm glad you're good."

Heat rose on his neck, flushing his face from jawline to forehead. So he turned back to his bag and whispered under his breath, "I got a walking thesaurus for a roommate, and he doesn't care how I'm doing really. I'll have to remember to keep my conversations to five words or less."

A fuzzy brown fleece jumpsuit was the issued sleeping attire—it had been laid out nicely on his bed the night before. It also had the AUCV patch over the left breast. In this section of the permafrost vault, the whole AUCV was segmented enough that they could run heat to around 55-60 degrees Fahrenheit or 12.7-15.5 degrees Celsius in most sleeping berths and labs and the cafeteria. The first night, Jørn woke up cold, but he had spoken to one of the other seed techs, and they made sure he had another thick wool blanket. He spread the olive-green blanket over the top of the thick goose-down comforter.

At first, sleep eluded him. His mind raced at the research he was about to embark on, but his physical body was exhausted. He succumbed to just staring at a brown spot on the ceiling tile directly over his head. The pale-yellow nightlight cast shadows that played with his mind, and before long, his breathing shallowed and his eyes stayed closed, heavy from fatigue.

—

Jørn shot awake to a hulking Viking of a man standing over him, jostling him to get up. The clock read three a.m. in glowing red numbers. He rubbed his face as he swung his legs off the bed.

"Hey, new guy," Rutger said. "Something is going on."

He didn't hear any emergency alarms, so he looked up

to a red siren light above their door. The raspberry-colored bulb cover was dark. *Emergency?* Jørn thought, and almost laid his head back down on his pillow.

"What is going on? Is this some sort of initiation thing?"

"No, negative, ix-nay, nada. It's Goran. I heard some singing outside of our door, and when I went to look, it was Goran pacing around in the hall . . . barefoot. There's too much permafrost for bare feet. Believe me, I would know." He spread his lanky toes before putting a sock on his foot. "I know a lot of scientists and seed techs do things at crazy hours, but the singing made no sense, and he was carrying a potted plant. It was strange. I came back in here to get my boots on and wake you up."

"Uh-oh." Jørn swung his feet off the bed and slipped his boots on also. "I saw this yesterday. We all saw it yesterday. It's his meds. We probably need to get Kincaid or something."

"Okay. I'll wake Dr. Kincaid, and you go get Goran. We don't want him going all the way out of the vault into the elements dressed the way he is."

"Sounds good."

By the time Jørn had left his room, though, the hall had filled with more scientists and seed techs. A lot of the women's and men's berths had awoken to Goran singing.

Elli sidled up to Jørn. "What's going on?"

"Oh, I think Goran's meds are making him talk crazy again. Like what happened yesterday."

"I didn't know that happened yesterday!"

"It was after we were in the lab for a while. Dr. Kincaid adjusted his meds for that wound he got, and he was better. I'm sure it's fine. You can go back to bed if you want."

"Okay." Elli turned to Lovise. "It's nothing. Let's go get some sleep."

Jørn was taken aback for a moment. He didn't realize that Lovise and Elli were berth mates.

"What's that?" One of the seed techs pointed toward Goran's neck. Jørn turned back to the group as Goran tried to work the handle to get from the sleeping berths to the main hall. It was an odd sight, kind of like a sleep-walking raccoon pawing at a piece of trash. He couldn't work the handle.

"Goran," Kennet said, "let's go back to bed."

The hallway separating the men's and women's berths was crowded now, and Elli and Lovise had come back to where Jørn was standing.

Goran froze and turned to the group, eyes wide and mouth slightly parted. Green chlorophyll had oozed out of various orifices and was now crusted on the corners of his mouth and ears. The potted plant had coursed its way up to the wound on the back of his head. Blood dripped from the base of the pot onto the tile floor.

Salomon entered the hallway fully dressed. He had a solo room farthest from the main hall. Farthest from where Goran stood. But within seconds, Salomon pushed his way through the standing-room-only crowd toward him.

"What's going on here?" Salomon asked.

Kennet recounted the incoherent mumbling song that Goran woke everyone up to. Then Goran spoke. "Leave stuff up alone here and now."

"Okay, Goran," Salomon said. "Let's get you to Dr. Kincaid."

Salomon took a step forward and Goran turned slightly, pulling the potted plant toward him as if he were protecting a basketball from a playground bully. Soil and crimson liquid sloshed over the lip of the pot.

"You kind but not keeping nothing creep right this way folks," he said.

Jørn raised an eyebrow. He concluded the potted plant had coursed its way to the back of Goran's head, made connection with the wound, and was now living off his blood.

Jørn and Salomon moved around him, and Jørn physically recoiled when he saw what the seed tech was pointing at. A thin green vine was sticking out of Goran's bandage. It grew down his neck and underneath his shirt like ivy, leaves budding all along its stem.

"What is it?" Goran asked, petrified.

For a moment, the poor guy was lucid, terror coloring his face.

"Somebody get Kincaid!" Salomon whispered.

SIXTEEN:

"Help me, Jørn," Salomon said, reaching for Goran's bandage. As he gingerly unwound it, Jørn pulled it into a clump in his hands.

"Please not stuff being the on stuff," Goran begged. He sounded slightly panicked, and his hands were pressed so hard against the pot that his fingertips were turning white.

"More plant," Salomon said.

"More *plant*?" Jørn repeated.

The terror was evident in his voice, and he couldn't deny that he also felt scared and uneasy. While the plant posed no threat to him—at least he didn't think so—it did potentially pose a threat to Goran. He'd hate to see the seed tech die because an unknown plant was growing inside his head. And it wasn't just medication making the man speak gibberish.

Salomon finished unwrapping the bandage, and Jørn tossed it aside. Part of Goran's head had been shaved so Kincaid could see the wound better. The skin around the wound was still pink, and drops of blood oozed out the edge. It wasn't hard to miss the green stem attached from the bloody wound to the potted plant.

A few of the seed techs recoiled. Kennet appeared, camera looped around his neck, and immediately began snapping pictures from all angles of Goran's head and the plant in the pot.

"Insane," he said. "You know how much these pictures are gonna be worth?"

"Kennet," Salomon said. "Not now."

Ignoring Salomon's words, Kennet leaned closer to Goran. "Just a few more pictures. I swear that's all I need."

Then it happened all at once.

Goran stared forward at the hallway full of scientists, his face a sickly white, his eyes bloodshot with terror, and then he looked up, lips trembling, and opened his mouth. *"Help me."*

A thick, dark vine shot out of Goran's mouth. Jørn screamed, tripping over himself, and fell on his back. The vine impaled the camera lens and went straight through Kennet's face. Jørn and Salomon were knocked to the floor, and a vine pinned them against the door exiting the berth. A fountain of blood erupted from where Kennet was impaled, splashing the scientists. Screams erupted in the hall. They reacted instantly and turned to run.

Everyone was tripping over each other until Salomon yelled over the chaos, "Everyone lock yourselves in your rooms!" Jørn didn't move. He couldn't move.

Two more vines as thick as an index finger thrust out of Goran's eyes, piercing Kennet through the chest. Blood spilled from both of the seed techs. Jørn raised his arm over his head and covered his face as a fine mist of blood fell upon him.

"Salomon!"

Jørn didn't see who shouted the name, but he was closest to the monstrosity, petrified by what he saw.

In an explosion of blood, a clump of vines ripped open the rest of Goran's face, sending scraps of skin and bone splattering against the walls. Suddenly free from the vine, Jørn scrambled to his feet and ran down the hall away from the thing.

Within an instant, the two seed techs were sewn together like a bastard quilt created by Mother Nature herself. Goran and Kennet, or what was left of them, writhed under the thickening blanket of leafy vine stems. Everyone stood silent as doors cracked opened so scientists could peek out at what had just happened.

A faint gurgle from air bubbling through a thick mixture of blood and chlorophyll interrupted the silence through the sleeping berths. The two seed techs became one, the vines creating a cocoon with the filleted and broken men inside.

Sobbing emerged from the crowd. The sound came from another seed tech whom Jørn hadn't met yet. A couple of scientists hugged the woman, trying to calm her. But how could they? What they had just witnessed was unworldly—certainly worth getting upset over. Jørn's stomach contracted, threatening to expel last night's dinner.

The two seed techs who were sewn together appeared to be dead. He hoped and prayed that was the case.

A vine as thick as Jørn's thigh split open the top of Goran's skull and swiveled around in the air. The tip of it bent in Salomon's direction.

Searching in slow, undulating movements.

"Salomon!" Jørn yelled, but the lead scientist couldn't hear him. The vine darted forward, and just as it was about to pierce Salomon, Lovise appeared, grabbed him by his coat, and yanked him backward. He fell, and the vine shot past right where he'd been standing.

The vine curled down, now pointed at Jørn. Before he could react, it lunged at him, but somebody had grabbed him by the shoulders and pulled him away, just as the tip of the vine impaled the carpeted floor, leaving a hole. *That's some serious force!* He looked up to see his rescuer. It was Elli.

Heart thudding in his chest and blood roaring in his ears, Jørn leaped to his feet and ran away from the two dead seed tech's bodies and the monstrous plant feasting on them.

The vine slinked like a cobra ready to strike and seemed to *look* around, as if sensing something in that narrow hallway.

Everyone from seed techs to scientists to medical staff stopped moving, all of them hoping it couldn't really see them.

When it could find no living person within ten feet, it turned back to what was left of Kennet. Slowly, it snaked into his ear, forcing the ear canal to widen until it split open the side of his head.

Clear brain fluid and dark pink spongy brain tissue the color of cherry Jell-O oozed onto the floor. There was more blood than Jørn thought possible. It soaked the floor, cascading under open dorm room doors. The green of the plant was now covered in red, and Jørn didn't even have to look down at himself to know the blood had covered him too.

A few more vines exploded out of Goran's body and slid into Kennet's like a surgeon placing a drain tube. Slowly, the plant tightened, and the two seed techs were brought closer together until they looked like they were permanently melded. The plant grew, slowly expanding over the bodies. While this happened, everybody in the berth watched, yet nobody made a sound, nobody moved. It was like they'd all been frozen.

Eventually, the bodies disappeared under a green

membrane. The plant metamorphosed into a giant cocoon-type specimen, its base slowly rising and falling as if it were breathing.

"What are all of you doing?" Salomon's gray hair was disheveled, and his face was sunken like he'd just aged ten years. His usual jovial tone was gone, replaced by a stern, hurried one. "Arm yourselves!" he said, spit flying from his lips.

The men's and women's berths went into a frenzy as people grabbed lamps and chairs out of their rooms, turning seemingly ordinary items into makeshift weapons.

Jørn found himself unable to move. He stood in the corner, Elli still by his side. They were among the ones standing the farthest away from the man-eating plant.

"Are you all right?" Elli asked, grabbing Jørn's face and pulling it close to hers. "Did it get you?"

"No, no, I'm all right." Jørn shook his head, but the words seemed to come from a distance, as if he wasn't actually the one saying them.

"I think you're in shock," she said, tapping his left cheek with her right hand. He could barely feel her touch, could barely understand the gravity of the situation. He knew he was supposed to feel something more than . . . blankness.

"Stick through this with me," Elli said. "You sure you're okay?"

He nodded because that's what he felt like he should do.

"We'll get you through this," she told him reassuringly, still smiling.

Salomon approached them and pressed something into both their hands. Fixed-blade survival knives with paracord handles, from his room. Jørn held the flat of the blade away from himself. He held out his arms and realized that he was covered in a thick layer of gore and bits of plants.

Rutger dragged a wooden desk chair into the hall and ripped off each of the four legs, then he broke the wrist-sized legs over his massive knee and handed the sharp splintered stick to Jørn and others in the hall. A shivering, wispy seed tech dropped the hair dryer she held like a gun and accepted the obviously more suitable weapon.

"Be ready to kill no matter what," Salomon said. Then he walked away.

SEVENTEEN:

Salomon was the first to approach the plant. It lay in an undulating heap on the floor. He reached out with a fire axe he'd retrieved from the back of the hallway and touched its butt to the plant.

Aside from its breathing-like movements, the plant didn't react.

Everyone's eyes were transfixed on the atrocity. The one coherent thought Jørn could form was that he was certain nobody else really understood the situation. It felt like a fever dream, like something that would be forgotten within the next few minutes because it simply couldn't be real.

Salomon stepped back and grabbed a desk lamp out of one of the seed techs' hands. He tossed it like a frisbee, and it bounced off the plant.

A low gurgling sound erupted from somewhere within the cocoon, and then the plant stopped moving altogether. Everyone took an involuntary step back. A couple of seed techs shielded their faces, ready for another attack.

"Is it . . . is it dead?" Asta asked. She was in the front line of the circle of scientists surrounding this thing. Her bracelet slid down her arm when she raised a fire extinguisher above her head.

"I don't know," Salomon said. "I don't think so . . ."

Jørn's nerves were finally calming. The gravity of the situation was settling in. He was able to look at the blood on his clothes, understand where it had come from, and not panic.

"What is it?" someone else asked.

That was the question of the day. It was clearly a massive carnivorous plant, but Jørn knew for certain that nothing like this had ever been recorded. Man-eating plants were something out of fiction, out of musicals. They weren't real, just as much as Superman wasn't real. Yet what they were looking at seemed very real. Did the scientists' experimentations go horribly wrong? Did they accidentally make something akin to a Venus flytrap on the scale of a human that also happened to have an appetite for human blood? Judging by the faces of everyone in the berth, the answer was no. If an experiment had gone this wrong, somebody would know.

"I don't think it's . . . breathing anymore," Lovise said. She was on the other side of the hall, pointing a putter toward it.

"We need to move it," Salomon said.

A chorus of uproars followed that statement, and it took him a solid two minutes to get everyone to calm down again.

"We'll loop some ropes around it and drag it to the lab. That way, we can all keep a safe distance. Let's also gather some more weapons, preferably axes, and get some gallons of gasoline and some matches. If this thing starts attacking us, we can torch it."

"We shouldn't be getting anywhere *near* it," Asta argued.

"I'm in charge here," Salomon said. "We need to dissect it. It's obviously mutated from the small plant you studied."

"But—"

Salomon raised his hand. "No buts here. We'll do as I say."

—

Forty minutes later, Jørn finally felt back to normal, if there even was such a thing, and every person in the vault was now gathered in the labs. He and Elli had a front-row seat, courtesy of Salomon.

There was a chilling quiet in the room. Two men had just been killed, two men who still had most of their lives to live. Everyone had seen them get viciously ripped apart, and yet nobody acknowledged it. Was it too disturbing to talk about? Was it something that everyone would simply choose to forget in order to spare their minds the trauma of remembering it?

The mucus-covered cocoon was wrapped in a blue tarp, with ropes securing it. Salomon signaled Lovise to prod it with the putter. Not only did she poke the tarp, she whaled on it a couple of times to make sure it was still nonvital.

With Salomon's bidding, Elli cut the coarse rope and stepped back. Like a flower opening its petals, the blue tarp's edges flopped open and the cocoon lay exposed on the lab table. Jørn took a step forward, but was greeted with a limp vine sliding off the table and slopping crimson fluid onto the floor.

He jumped back. "For hell's sake!" His nerves were fried, and he couldn't calm himself enough to even get a good look at the thing. It was clearly dead.

Asta and Salomon attached several monitoring wires to the plant cocoon because they weren't treating this as a normal plant dissection, but an animal dissection. Many of the wires running to the thing were to read vitals, while some were leads with sticky electrode pads. And a couple were placed to fry the sucker if at any moment Salomon deemed it necessary.

"Are you sure you're okay being here?" Lovise asked. She sat next to Jørn, gripping his hand in hers. He liked her company, her presence; he felt safe around her.

"I need to see this," he told her. He meant it too. As shaken as he was, he needed answers. Those were the only things that could bring him peace.

"Exterminators," Salomon said, holding the button to trigger electrical shock, "stand ready." He and Asta took three steps back, while ten men took three steps forward. They had each traded their makeshift bedroom-furniture weapons and brandished deadlier ones—sharp swords, chainsaws, axes, blowtorches.

"We're ready boss, chief, leader, head honcho, captain."

Jørn didn't even have to turn to look to know that was Rutger.

"If this thing so much as moves," Salomon said, "I'm going to shock it, and if it tries to attack again, you guys torch it, chop it, and cut it to pieces."

For a second, Jørn wondered if they should torch the thing now to be safe. Screw the studies and the science. This thing had just killed two people. But before he could speak his mind, Salomon pressed the button.

The whole of the plant lurched upward in a sharp motion, but went still just as fast. Salomon shocked it again and again, but each time, the plant showed no signs of movement aside from its nerves firing off from the jolt of electricity.

They waited a few moments in silence, and then Salomon waved away the crew of armed men and stepped back up to the plant.

Asta squinted at a monitor and scribbled the findings in a mottled-green lab notebook.

"It is my conclusion that this thing has expired," Salomon said, staring it up and down. "Whatever *it* is."

"Dead," Elli whispered.

Jørn nodded.

In one swift movement, Salomon raised a clenched fist and punched the plant as hard as possible. A wet *slap* resounded through the lab.

Jørn flinched and squinted. His upper lip raised, and he felt conflicted. *Did Salomon just punch Kennet's and Goren's corpses?* Lovise must have felt his unease—she gripped his hand tighter.

Salomon pulled his hand away, glaring at his swelling knuckles. "Let's start the dissection."

EIGHTEEN:

Asta handed a diamond-sharpened surgical blade to Jørn, like a proud parent passing the turkey-carving knife to their firstborn. He stepped forward and faltered.

"What's the matter?" she asked, holding the scalpel out.

"Should I really be doing this?" he whispered. "I mean, I'm just an intern." Suddenly he felt all eyes on him.

Asta leaned in. "But you're the only mechanobiologist we have. And who else would understand this more and be able to navigate a complex plant species dissection?"

Just then, he felt a hand on his shoulder. Their private conversation had ended.

"I know you think you don't have the experience, but you're our resident mechanobiologist," Salomon said. "It wasn't an accident that I invited you and Elli here. You have the knowledge we need in cellular mechanotransduction, tissue engineering, disease mechanobiology, and biomechanics, right?"

Jørn nodded slowly. Salomon's words seemed to soothe his nerves and inject him with the confidence needed to perform. Plus, he'd be able to be on the forefront of all the research of this new species if he didn't back down.

Jørn took the surgical blade from Asta and pressed it against the plant's husk. The transparent husk had a hue of pale green with overtones of crimson red, making the whole thing look like a human-sized rotting hot dog. The pod had fully grown veins coursing through, and Jørn could see that blood had occupied the lumen of each vessel. He made sure he made his cut in between two thick arteries. The first cut was harder than he thought. The husk was thick and slippery. Eventually, he resorted to stabbing the tip of the knife into the skin to start the incision. In the end, the initial incision was less finesse and more sawing back and forth as if it were a gelatin log.

As he cut it open, blood spilled out over the edge of the counter and onto the lab floor, splashing shoes. No one moved. They all stood firm and ready to destroy it if needed. Jørn tried to justify why Salomon wanted to dissect it instead of just destroying it, but then scientific intrigue and wonder pushed the question aside.

As he cut through it, Jørn allowed himself a closer look at the plant. Thick, full veins coursed along the outside membrane, and green chlorophyll excretion dripped from random parts of the husk. Jørn *was* fascinated. Two emotions battled for first place in his head. It was the most disgusting thing he'd witnessed, yet he wanted to work up to his elbows in the dissection field all afternoon long. They were witnessing something never seen by any other human.

Jørn finally tore the rest of the way through the plant—there was no easy way of doing it—then Asta and Salomon each grabbed one side of the opening and peeled back its firm, thick membrane, revealing its innards.

A socked foot flopped out of the opening and hung

limply before splatting to the floor. Rutger stabbed it with the sharp end of his desk chair leg "just in case it was alive." A few people recoiled; one seed tech ran out of the room. Jørn merely swallowed hard, staving off the urge to vomit.

Asta slowly lifted the foot and set it aside. It had been severed mid-shin, and splintered white bone stuck out, a stark contrast to the shredded muscle surrounding it. Jørn made a mental note to never cook or eat ham hocks again.

She placed the foot on the counter, and another seed tech Jørn didn't know stepped forward and began taking pictures. Kennet's old job.

"Scalpel," Asta said, holding out her open hand.

Jørn was happy to take the assisting role at the moment as he took in the entire scene. He handed her one, and she reached inside the opening and began slicing through another layer with surgical precision. Every inch or so, a bubble of green ooze would grow until it popped, squirting a chlorophyllic blood mixture, barely missing their goggled faces.

"Salomon," Asta said, waving him over.

Despite how haggard Salomon appeared, he moved with ageless speed. Peering over the opening Asta had made, he only spent half a minute examining whatever lay on the inside before pointing at Jørn. "You're probably more equipped than any of us here to understand what's going on."

The inside was dark blood floating on puddles of green excretion like an oil slick on the surface of water. The stench of copper and fresh-cut grass filled the air. Jørn held the back of his hand up to his nose.

He'd gone into plant biology because plants were only slightly unpredictable, because there was virtually no risk for people who stared at leaves all day. Yet here he was, staring into the innards of the most fascinating, frightening, unpredictable thing on Earth.

The first thing he saw was a partially dissolved body. He thought it was Kennet's, but he couldn't be sure. *Poor Kennet.* The face was destroyed beyond recognition. The seed tech's body was torn wide open, and small green veins wrapped around the man's organs and had traveled most of the way through his own veins.

"The plant is acting as a parasite," Jørn said, even though he suspected Asta and Salomon already knew that. "I can't imagine an environmental scenario drastic enough to transform a plant's biology on this scale. It looks like a plant, even acts like a plant to an extent, but it's simultaneously carnivorous and parasitic."

With a sudden urge of confidence and curiosity, Jørn pulled away from the plant and found a box of new gloves. He slipped some on, ignoring the crowd's stares, and returned to the plant.

He stuck his hands in, moving aside tendrils and unrecognizable organ masses, his fingers lapping through puddles of liquid. The plant was triple the size of a regular human being, and its inside was nearly as vast.

He found the second body without a problem.

"I assumed wrong," Jørn proclaimed. "The first body is Goran." He held up a name badge from the second body. Drops of a viscous green-red substance coursed down the front, revealing Kennet's smiling face in the small photo. Jørn wiped the rest of the fluid with his thumb to confirm that the second body belonged to him.

He set the ID on the table next to the plant mass and kept probing. Up until now, most everything in the plant's cavity was soft, including the bones, but when his hands landed on something hard, he ripped it free from the inside of the capsule's wall. Though destroyed beyond any hope of usefulness, Kennet's camera was hard to miss. Jørn didn't realize the strap was still around the cervical vertebra, and when he dislodged the camera, he dislodged Kennet's head, causing it to rise to the top of the pile of plant and guts.

A single eye hung from its optic nerve, dangling from Kennet's shredded eye socket. Jørn reached out to touch it, but flinched when the eye *moved* and the pupil dilated.

"Scalpel," Jørn said, and the moment he reached out his hand, someone pressed it into his palm.

He grabbed the eyeball, felt it moving beneath his fingers, then severed it from its sinew-laden optic nerve. He had to saw back and forth, not once, not twice, but three times. And each time, he felt a bubble in his stomach rise. A spurt of runny green sludge splashed his goggles, as if someone threw a rotten egg at his face. Jørn flinched back, trying to dodge the slime, to no avail. One of the seed techs gasped, then fainted. A handful of scientists tended to him.

But through it all, he saw two vines wriggling desperately, as if they were searching for something new to latch on to.

He stepped away again and placed the eyeball on the counter.

"It's still alive," he said. "Partially, at least."

A groan rippled through the audience. Rutger and two more seed techs stepped forward with weapons drawn.

"It's okay," Jørn said. "This is Kennet's eye. I severed it from the optic nerve. The plant definitely reacted, if only slightly. Must've been using it to take in its environment, to look at us."

Salomon grabbed Jørn's shoulder. He was so much taller, but at that moment, Jørn felt Salomon was just as small as him. There was something about watching two men get brutally murdered by a plant that reduced them down to the smallest versions of themselves.

"Thank you, Jørn. I think . . . I think you need some rest. I think we all do."

"Don't leave this thing unattended," he said. "We might wake up in the morning to find ourselves living in a bloody jungle."

"I'll make sure it's contained," Salomon said, managing a half smile, "until we can run some more tests. For now, let's get some sleep."

"I don't think I'll sleep anyway." Jørn lay the scalpel on a silver tray. "Let's finish this tonight and dispose of it. What if it somehow repairs itself?"

"We've discovered something that will be studied for decades to come." Salomon rubbed his eyes. "What we do tonight will follow us for the rest of our lives. Precision is imperative. We cannot afford to make a careless mistake. Sleep-deprived people make stupid errors."

Jørn nodded. He knew he needed to be away from all this. Part of him understood the shock had yet to wear off, but the other part of him was scared to be alone.

Before he could take one step, Lovise was by his side, looping her arm through his. "Come on, Jørn."

He didn't say anything. Instead, he let her guide him through the vault, passing the countless pairs of wide eyes watching them as they went.

She took him to the men's berth and helped him sit on his bed. His internal clock was blaring, agitating, warning him this wasn't a good time to go to sleep. He hated the idea of that *thing* being unattended, no matter how secure the room it was housed in.

Lovise helped him out of his clothes, disappeared for

a moment, returned with a hot, wet rag, and began rubbing at parts of his skin.

She's rubbing the blood off. But the thought was too far away to make much sense at all.

When Lovise was done, she helped him into bed.

Before she could leave, he grabbed her hand. "Stay with me?" he asked, even though he wasn't sure the words even left his mouth.

She nodded, stripped the soiled jumpsuit off her lithe frame—Jørn only noticed just then how much blood her clothes were covered in—and climbed under the covers with him.

"Let's shower first," he said.

Lovise raised an eyebrow.

"Not together." Jørn raised his hands, stumbling over his words. "I mean, the blood . . . let's just be sure we've rid it from our bodies, okay?"

"Yeah, good idea." Lovise touched her red hair. "Meet you back here in ten?"

Jørn nodded. Before he knew it, he was watching red water circle a drain by his feet. He'd always been practical, studying plants since he was a teenager—with little interest in dating. Heck, he'd barely kissed a girl before he set off for Antarctica, and now, he'd been bold enough to invite a girl into his bed. Maybe it was the adrenaline . . . or maybe it was something that Lovise had awakened in him.

After toweling off and returning to his bed, he was asleep before he understood that he was sharing a bed with the most beautiful girl he had ever seen.

NINETEEN:

Jørn's dreams were hyper-violent and involved bleeding plants and screaming people. He slept fitfully, and when he awoke, he was vaguely aware that his sleep hadn't been decent at all. He was more exhausted than when he went to bed.

He opened his eyes to find that Lovise was not lying next to him. When he checked his watch, he wasn't surprised. He'd slept for far longer than was deemed average.

He pushed himself up in bed. He was still in his floral boxers.

Jørn got out of bed and fished through his bags until he found sweats and a T-shirt. His neglect of formal uniform was intentional. He didn't intend to go back to the labs for quite some time.

By the time he was dressed and considering what to do next, someone knocked on his door.

"Come in," he said, dreading the upcoming social interaction.

But it was Elli who poked her head in. "Hi, Jørn," she said softly. "Do you want some food?"

"What time is it?" he asked.

"Twenty-one-hundred hours," she said. "You slept for some time."

"I could use some food, yeah," he said.

"Be right back," she said before shutting the door.

As much as Jørn tried not to think about the man-eating plant, he couldn't avoid it. Seeing that thing rip through Goran and Kennet was emblazoned like a cattle brand on his brain—he would never be able to forget it.

Was his theory correct? He'd cut out Kennet's eye and deemed that the plant was still alive. But he had no proof aside from an eye dilating and moving. After all, they were dealing with something unknown. If he was right, was their safety under threat? Or had the plant reached some kind of stasis? Had it consumed enough human flesh that it was satisfied with its current state? All he knew was that it needed to be exterminated.

It was hard to come to any conclusions without studying the subject, or at the very least without having some sort of report on it, so he did the only thing he could that would keep him as far away from the monster as possible: He dug out his books on every genus of plant and began to read.

As was obvious, the plant shared similarities with carnivorous and parasitic plants. It wasn't unheard of for either class of plant to grow inside humans before, but at this level, it had to be one of the two.

Theoretically, plants could grow in blood. Blood, after all, contained nitrogen, potassium, and phosphorous—nitrogen being the most important. And those were the three main things plants needed to survive. But again, nothing explained the rapid growth.

It *had* to be genetically modified. It was the only viable solution. Even if it hadn't been modified in the vault's lab, it had been modified somewhere else. *But who sent it here?* It was the only thing that made sense.

He studied for only twenty minutes before Elli

knocked on the door again. This time, she didn't wait for a response. She stepped inside, carrying a tray of sandwiches.

"The schedule had them serving stew, but I don't think anybody was up for that for obvious reasons."

She set the tray down next to Jørn on the bed. He picked up half a sandwich. Turkey with mayo, tomato, brown deli mustard, and cheese. Of course, they'd left off the lettuce. Nobody wanted to be reminded of plants right now.

"How's everyone else holding up?" Jørn asked.

"Better than expected," Elli said around a mouthful of food. "Salomon thinks we're all experiencing some kind of group shock. I don't think any of it has really settled in." She paused, blinked, then went back to her food.

"Any news on the . . . on the thing?"

"Hasn't moved," she said. "Not since you had a look at it."

"Good," Jørn said. "Maybe it really is dead."

"I've been telling Salomon they need to burn it. Why risk more lives in the name of research?"

"Some people would say that's a noble cause to die for," Jørn said. Elli shot him a harsh look. "I agree with you. Yes, they should torch the thing. But I understand why Salomon wants to get some notes on the discovery first. He's head of one of the world's foremost leading labs on plant research. In his eyes, he'd look like a coward for giving up this easily."

"It killed two people, Jørn!"

"I know. I'm broken up about that."

"What should we do, then?" Elli asked.

"I get that Salomon wants to study it, probably write some papers about it or something. But honestly, we need to get everyone to safety. We don't know what it is. We don't know what it wants. I don't want to risk anyone else. Oh no! I just realized."

Elli stared at him. "What?"

"Dr. Miller had the same thing. We need to tell Salomon to go check on him and then I'm going to recommend that we all get out of here."

"That's the most reasonable thing. I agree with you." Elli finished her sandwich, then sat, staring at the wall. "That thing moved so fast. If it isn't dead, and it attacks again, I don't know if we'll be able to stop it."

"I never told you," Jørn said as he continued nibbling at his sandwich, "thank you for saving me."

She looked at him blankly.

"For pulling me away when it was attacking Goran and Kennet. Thank you. I couldn't move. I . . . froze or something."

"No need to thank me, that's what friends do," Elli said. "You were in shock. We came here together, we're leaving together. Besides, I hope you'll repay the favor if the time comes for it."

TWENTY:

Lovise stayed in Jørn's room again that night. Despite sleeping and studying textbooks most of the day, neither had trouble falling asleep.

Jørn woke before Lovise. The clock told him it was 7:15 a.m. He felt better than he had the day before, but not by much. He sighed and sat up in bed.

Lovise was curled against the wall. The bed creaked when he sat up, and she opened her eyes.

"How are you?" she asked. Jørn had never seen her like this: Her hair was messy and uncombed, her eyes were a bit swollen from the stress of everything and likely not enough sleep, and her lips were dry. A desire to see her like this again surged up inside of him, but he ignored it.

"Fine," he told her. "I want to go home."

She nodded. "I bet everyone wants the same thing."

"We aren't supposed to see a chopper for another month." Jørn swung his legs off the bed and pinched his head between his hands. "But our pilot said they could come when there's an emergency. Is that true?"

"Yeah! That's right. We need to call and get them to come evacuate us. I think they will come if we radio them," Lovise said. She sat up, too, and began scratching Jørn's back. "Especially for an emergency! We can go talk to Salomon. I'm sure we won't be the first ones to ask him about it."

Lovise stood up and headed for the door. She was dressed in a baggy T-shirt and a pair of short shorts. Everything about her was alluring, and a warm, aggressive feeling erupted in his stomach.

"I'll go get ready. You do the same. We'll go talk to him together."

He nodded and looked away from her eyes. But his gaze naturally went to her legs. He looked back up, blushing, and she just smiled and left the room.

A half-hour later, once Jørn was showered, dressed, and ready to go, Lovise entered his room. She didn't knock this time, and he found that made him happy.

"Let's go," she said.

Together, they walked down the long hallway, passing only a few people who were also on their way to breakfast. When they emerged from the hallway and began walking to the cafeteria, Jørn found it uncharacteristically silent. It was nearly as busy as the day before, but nobody was talking. Everyone ate slowly and silently.

"Have you seen Salomon?" Lovise asked, grabbing a passing seed tech by his elbow.

The seed tech shook his head. "I don't think he's gotten up yet. But you may wanna check the lab."

Without a word, Jørn and Lovise left the cafeteria, ascended the steps, and turned in the direction of the lab.

She didn't say anything, and even though he wanted to talk to her, he couldn't think of anything to say. She was wearing the same thing as Jørn, the boring gray lab clothes the AUCV had provided them. She'd brushed her hair, and it fell loosely around her face.

As they passed the greenhouses, Jørn realized that this area was even quieter than the cafeteria. Was anyone even up here? Or was absolutely no one eager to see the monster plant in spite of the research Salomon wanted to do on it?

Lovise pushed open the door to the lab. The automatic lights flickered to life.

Jørn was glad he hadn't eaten breakfast, because his stomach immediately began lurching at what he smelled. Bitter fermented chlorophyllic blood covered the entirety of the lab. It dripped from the ceiling and the walls and was gathered in puddles on the floor. Chemistry glassware had been broken and shards of beakers and flasks lay stuck in the sticky chlorophyll blood mixture. Masses of plant and meat—most likely human—were scattered about. Jørn stepped over a large gray-pink intestine to enter.

"It got someone else," Lovise said.

He nodded, stepping deeper into the lab, but keeping his head on a swivel, looking for any signs of movement, when he spotted half a hand still gripping the leg of a table.

"Do you see it anywhere?" Jørn whispered.

"No. I think it's gone."

"Go get Salomon!" he said. "I'll try to figure out where it went."

Lovise was gone without another word. Jørn grabbed an axe from the wall and steeled himself. There was a funny smell in the lab, one that he tried not to pay attention to. He was in the center of a blood bath. The plant had torn someone to shreds and devoured most of them.

The chlorophyll slime grew thicker the deeper the lab

went. Eventually, it formed into a trail, and Jørn slowly followed it to the back of the lab. Just as he reached its end, he heard a commotion behind him and turned around.

"This can't be happening!" It was Salomon who spoke. The lead scientist was disheveled. The top button of his shirt didn't align with the top hole, and his hair was matted on one side.

Lovise and Elli stood behind him, along with a few other seed techs Jørn didn't know.

"It somehow bore straight through the permafrost walls," Jørn said, stepping aside to reveal the gaping hole in the wall. The frost around it was stained red, and strands of hair stuck to the frozen blood. The plant had inexplicably eaten a hole in the wall and burrowed so deep that Jørn couldn't see the end.

"We should have torched that thing the other night!" he said.

"We need to figure out who the casualty was," Salomon replied. "Search for any identifying factors, like clothing, jewelry, or hair. Be on high alert."

Jørn took a moment to peer into the tunnel. A few feet in, it curved to the left. He couldn't see anything coming from it. Maybe the plant drilled itself outside the mountain and was now roaming free somewhere in Antarctica. It had probably burrowed back into the AUCV, but nobody had found it yet.

"I found something," Elli said. She lifted a bracelet into the air.

Jørn recognized it instantly. A Nepalese bracelet.

"Asta," Salomon said quietly. His face contorted, and he bit his lip, fighting back some tears.

"Let's get a team together," he continued, taking a

deep breath through his nose. "It's time to find that thing and kill it. Screw the research. We'll burn it to ash."

"Why didn't we burn it the other night?!" Jørn said.

"It wasn't deemed a threat then, Jørn," Salomon said. "We had dissected the thing past death and then some. I had Asta making notes on all of our findings and we were going to dispose of it this morning."

"But still," Jørn said. "Asta's dead, Goran's dead, Kennet's dead! How many more people need to die?"

"What do you think we're doing right now?" Salomon replied.

"Why do you think I'm here, Salomon?! I'm the first mechanobiologist to ever come through the AUCV. I want to study this thing more than anyone here. But enough is enough."

"Right! That's why we are going to kill it! Haven't I made myself clear?"

"Right," Jørn repeated, "okay! Yeah. We're on the same page, then."

Salomon put a hand on his shoulder and smiled. "We've always been on the same page."

"Great," he said. "We need to call the mainland."

Salomon turned to one of the seed techs. "Viggo, go tell Miller to get the chopper here! He needs to make it clear that the entire Avling Universal Crop Vault will be evacuated! Go! Now!"

Viggo turned on a dime, slipped on the permafrost ground, then found his footing and carefully jogged toward Dr. Miller's room.

TWENTY-ONE:

Jørn volunteered to be the first to go through the tunnel. Salomon armed him with an axe, informing him that he'd sent a seed tech to fuel the flamethrowers. Why the AUCV had flamethrowers was beyond Jørn's imagination, but he liked the idea of wielding one against the man-eating plant.

Lovise didn't come. Neither did Elli, as she had opted to stay back and help clean up the lab with several other seed techs. Jørn could tell she was upset about Asta's death. She stood on the fringe of the group, holding herself, arms crossed in front of her, as she stared at an assay machine that had been toppled by the plant creature. Jørn wanted to stay to comfort her, but he concluded that finding the plant was more important.

Salomon followed right behind Jørn, and a dozen other seed techs were behind him. They'd entered the tunnel only moments ago, and Jørn was just rounding the first corner. The walls were slimed with the same chlorophyll-blood residue left behind in the lab. The floor was slippery, and he struggled to balance.

"Everybody quiet," Salomon hissed, motioning to the seed techs behind him.

The tunnel, now shrouded in silence only interrupted by quiet footsteps, was much eerier than before.

Jørn strained his ears to listen, but heard nothing ahead of them. Unless the plant was remaining entirely still, it wasn't nearby.

Salomon had given everybody headlamps, and Jørn found he was much more confident going forward when it wasn't total darkness in front of him.

They rounded another corner of the tunnel. It was shrinking, as if the plant had gotten tired and bored the hole smaller as it went. Nobody besides Salomon had to crouch, but even he only had to bend slightly.

The residue was getting thinner, too, as the tunnel went on.

Jørn felt dizzy and sick with fear and nerves. He needed to stay focused while also forcing himself to think of anything other than what he was doing. He made himself think about Lovise, about the nights they'd spent together. It would have been wildly more exciting for him in any other circumstance, and while it did make his heart beat faster, and his palms start to sweat, he wished it hadn't happened under these circumstances. Was she just being kind to him because she was worried about him? Or was she acting this way because she was scared, and he was a new distraction in her life? He'd be a fool to dismiss how much the events played a part in it.

If the plant hadn't torn three people to shreds, there was no chance their newly-formed friendship would have escalated to this level. So when they got back home, would things stay the same, or would they lose touch? Nothing more than a fling.

The thought of never seeing her in pajamas or without makeup or never sharing a close personal space with her again made him deeply sad.

Did Lovise even like him? Nothing overtly romantic had happened. They hadn't shared their feelings or kissed. They'd just held each other after a traumatic event. Jørn's instinct was to believe that, but something told him this was different. While horrific circumstances had forced them together, there was a spark with Lovise that he felt almost instantly after they met. He cursed himself again for putting his love life on the back burner when he should have been dating like everyone else. His lack of experience was now a glaring oversight in the résumé of his life.

Jørn shook his head. He was calm enough again to focus back on the task at hand.

The tunnel had gone straight for a long time, but was curving again. Jørn had always had a solid sense of direction, and he knew they would soon be emerging into another part of the AUCV.

"Do you see the light?" Salomon whispered.

He did. It was a bluish hue that barely seeped into the tunnel, a thinning of the tunnel wall and the AUCV. Jørn gripped higher on the axe and held it up to his shoulder. If he had to, he was ready to swing.

They reached the end of the tunnel. He pressed his back against the wall and steadied his breathing, watching plumes of frozen breath rise lazily to the ceiling.

"What do you see?" Salomon asked.

Jørn peered around the corner. "The Box. It breached The Box!"

The plant had bored through the side of the mountain all the way to the opposite end of the AUCV just to reach the seed vault.

"I don't think it's in here," Jørn said, stepping in.

Salomon nodded and waved the seed techs forward. One by one, they all piled through. Jørn went last.

The Box was in pretty decent shape. He had expected the place to be a disaster, but from the trails of slimy chlorophyllin residue, it looked like the plant had simply moved around all the tables and shelves. A few of the boxes housing seeds were ripped apart, and it looked like the plant had ingested some of them, but other than that, there was minimal damage.

"What was it after?" Jørn asked.

"I'm not sure if it was after anything," Salomon said. "Might be some instinctual thing. It attacked Goran here first, and maybe it wanted to return here for whatever reason."

One of the seed techs found the light switch. The lights flickered on, though it didn't reveal anything their headlamps hadn't already.

"Remind me to access the import logs," Salomon said. "I want to look for red flags. See if I can't find out which country sent us this thing—if anyone did."

Jørn nodded and pulled some vials from his pockets. They'd come with two missions: kill the plant if they located it and collect whatever evidence they could find. He went to each box of seeds that'd been broken open and collected samples from there. Then he began working on scooping up some of the chlorophyll. He doubted it was any different than what they'd found in the lab, but it was better to be safe.

Minutes later, one of the seed techs called attention to the wall. A streak of heme-chlorophyll mixture rose to a vent duct.

"How did it fit in there?" Jørn asked, realizing this was where the plant had gone.

"It must be able to alter its size somehow—like an octopus," Salomon said. "We need to alert everyone. The plant is now in the vents. It could attack anywhere at any time."

TWENTY-TWO:

They all gathered in the lab. Everyone in the AUCV, including the cooks, janitors, nurses, seed techs, Dr. Miller, Salomon, and a couple of maintenance guys Jørn had never seen before.

It'd taken half the day to locate most of the pieces from Asta's corpse. A hand here and a mandible there. One of the seed techs even took it upon himself to find all of her missing teeth littered amongst the broken chemistry glass and upended machines. The janitors had placed Asta's remaining body parts in an old cooler so her family would have something to bury later. What was odd was it didn't try to grow *in* her like it had with Kennet and Goran; her body was free of any sprouts.

They'd vowed to begin searching the vents later, but Salomon had insisted they get everyone in the same room and explain what was going on. He'd ordered everyone to always travel in pairs and always travel with weapons. Then, for the sake of simplicity, he'd said the man-eating plant was now called Gnashvine. A fitting mash of two words to accurately describe the chlorophyllic creature.

The cooks had brought out a seemingly bottomless supply of alcohol, and most everyone was sipping full glasses of whiskey.

"I'm scared," Elli said. She and Jørn sat together with

their backs to a wall, certain the Gnashvine was now traveling exclusively through the vent systems. They both watched the vent across the room. It hadn't needed to be said—everyone was watching the vents. "I wish we were back at school."

"It'll be okay," he said, but his heart wasn't in the words.

"You don't know that," she said.

"I don't know that, yeah. But that's what I hope."

She turned to face him, but at that moment, Salomon interrupted them.

"Jørn," he said, his voice low, "will you do me a favor?"

Jørn nodded his head despite a desperate desire to do nothing else but sit with his classmate and let other people deal with the Gnashvine. Salomon clearly trusted him, and more than likely needed him.

"Will you go with Lovise to the equipment room and bring back a list of things I gave her? There should be a cart. You can just pile everything on that and roll it back here."

"You're not worried the plant is there?" Jørn asked.

"The *Gnashvine*, Jørn," Salomon corrected. "And no. There are no vents leading to that room. Just take an axe with you to be safe."

"Salomon?" Elli said.

"Yes?"

"Were you able to make contact with the mainland about a helicopter rescue?"

"Yes, of course. I sent Viggo earlier. Dr. Miller is waiting for the estimated time of arrival and will let all of you know when we can get out of here."

"Is he . . . okay? No vines growing out of his head?"

"Yes, yes, we've been monitoring him closely. I'll let

you know when I know." Salomon walked away. Jørn watched him, and then paused when he saw Lovise by the lab entrance. She smiled at him.

Then he got up and left.

—

Lovise ran her fingers through her long red hair, letting it drop around her slender shoulders as they walked cautiously down the hallway to the supplies area. Her lab coat was open, and she wore creased dress pants and a white button-up shirt. Not the drab jumpsuit some of the other more permanent scientists wore under their coats.

Jørn kept his eyes ahead. He gripped the axe and held it, ready to swing. He wasn't particularly concerned about the plant. He imagined it was impossible for it to remain silent, so they would hear it long before they saw it.

"So," Lovise said, her brown eyes scanning the hallway. "What's up with you and that Elli girl?"

Discomfort spiked through Jørn. He'd been worried about this—Lovise asking about Elli.

A door labeled "MAINTENANCE" came into view.

"We went to grad school together," he said. "Didn't go into the same field, obviously, but we had a lot of classes together, and we were in the same social circles. A bunch of us applied for the positions at the AUCV. She got in, of course. She was the smartest of all of us. I got accepted because of my studies in mechanobiology."

"Okay," Lovise said. They'd reached the door to the maintenance room. "I guess that's a story, but it's not what I asked for."

Jørn thought back to all the times he'd thought about Elli *like that*. It was so stupid, so obvious now. You could appreciate the beauty of a rose, but that didn't mean you should date it. Elli was a beautiful, friendly rose. "We're friends. Actually, maybe good friends. But nothing more than that."

"I can see that. She's a cool girl." Lovise pushed open the door. "Just figured I better check first." The automatic lights flickered on, and Jørn went in first, brandishing his axe.

It was evident the Gnashvine wasn't there and never had been. The room was free of chlorophyll and slime, and everything seemed to be in place. It was a spacious area with rows of shelves lining the walls. Something giant sat in the center of the room, covered by a tarp.

"That's a boring drill," Lovise said, pointing to the tarp. "It's how they dug out the tunnels to build this place."

"Why is it here?" Jørn asked.

"Never bothered to take it out, I guess," Lovise said. "Hauling equipment to and from here is really expensive, I suppose. It might have been cheaper to just never send it back."

She pulled a folded list out of her pocket and began reading it. "Let's first start by arming ourselves with anything that will burn. Then we'll focus on some specific fertilizer ingredients." She squinted at the list. "I think he wants to brew some pesticides or explosives or something."

Jørn set down his axe and began making his way across the room to where more flamethrowers hung on the wall.

"Hold on," Lovise said. She grabbed his hand and pulled him to a stop. "I want to try something."

She grabbed the back of his neck, studied his face for a moment, and then pulled him in for a kiss. Now he understood what she meant by checking first.

TWENTY-THREE:

Their lips met. He froze, his heart hammering in his chest, blood rushing through his body. It felt good to kiss her. Then his hands found her waist. He wasn't sure if it was the whiskey, the stress, or infatuation, but he leaned in for more.

They stumbled backward, both her hands in his hair, both of his running up and down her body. He crashed into a shelf, and a few items fell to the ground, clanging at an unusually quiet volume.

With his back against the shelves, she wrapped her legs around him. He pulled her in closer.

"You smell so good," she whispered as her mouth moved along his jaw.

His thoughts were racing with plant-based puns, but for the first time ever, he didn't have a problem pushing them out of his mind.

Her hands moved to the collar of his shirt, and as she moved to take it off, Jørn lost his balance, and they fell to the floor.

For a second, he was concerned he'd killed the moment, but she began to laugh. It was loud and slightly obnoxious, but it was the nicest sound he'd heard in days.

She rolled on top of him, shedding her white coat, and they continued to kiss.

"I like you," Lovise said between kisses. "I like you, a lot."

Her wandering hands moved to the buttons of her shirt. She began undoing them, and Jørn's stomach lurched.

"I like you too," he said, his hands on her pulsing thighs.

Someone screamed.

It was faint, so distant that it could have been the squeaking hinge of a swinging door, but it was impossible to deny.

Jørn and Lovise froze.

They were breathing heavily, and they had to take a couple deep breaths in order to go quiet.

Another scream echoed from somewhere deep in the AUCV.

They jumped to their feet. Jørn paused for a moment, transfixed by Lovise.

Once they all got out of this, and once they were all back home, he would ask her out on a date. He straightened his clothing, and she put her lab coat back on.

"We might need these," she said, grabbing two flamethrowers off the wall and tossing one to him.

She opened the door and stepped out into the hallway while adjusting her collar.

"If I die," Jørn said, needing to lighten the fear in his gut, "thanks for *planting* one on me."

Lovise rolled her eyes. "You're not gonna die," she said. "Besides, we need to finish what we started in there. Can't leave me spending my whole life wondering how the rest of it would have gone."

His face went hot. She smiled at him, and then broke into a run down the hallway.

The screaming didn't come from the lab.

By the time Jørn and Lovise had reached the walkway leading to the lab, a clump of people had formed near the door to the cold greenhouse. It was open, and an icy chill blew from it.

Unable to push his way through the growing group of people, Jørn tried looking over everyone to see what was going on.

"Everyone back!" It was Dr. Miller. He stood in the door frame, pulling someone from the cold greenhouse. His stony face was now cinched into something resembling pain.

"Move!" he shouted again.

Everybody moved to make way for Dr. Miller. People's whispers became rushed, and then Jørn saw who it was.

It was Salomon!

Dr. Miller pulled his friend to the lab. Jørn grabbed Salomon's ankles and helped carry him. Everyone followed.

"What happened?" he asked.

Dr. Miller's response was just shaking his head.

They moved slowly to the lab. Once there, Dr. Miller and Jørn moved to a free table. Everyone continued whispering, and some held back tears. What had happened to their leader?

Jørn got the answer to his question when they heaved Dr. Salomon onto a lab bench. His small and large intestines looped lazily out of his gut from a large dark red gash the width of his pelvis. One of his arms had been ripped off, leaving frayed skin, mangled muscle, and jagged bone at the open stump. The last observation was deep gashes running along the side of his face. This wasn't like Goran's and Kennet's abomination.

"No!" Lovise yelled. She grabbed Jørn's arm.

"I know this comes as a shock to us all," Dr. Miller said. He was talking at a normal volume, but his voice boomed through the lab. "But we can't deny it now. This creature isn't going to stop. It's up to us to kill it before it kills anyone else."

"What was he doing in the cold greenhouse?" It was a random seed tech who asked the question.

"Retrieving supplies," Dr. Miller said. "He wanted to make some bombs and poison gases from fertilizer. From now on, we travel in pairs, no exceptions. Clearly, the thing is using the vents to get around, so don't linger near them. Also, find a weapon and keep it on you at all times."

"When will the helicopters get here?" a janitor asked. His eyes were wide open. Fear had begun to consume him. "If you won't force the issue, *I* will!"

"They're coming! We're at the mercy of the weather," Dr. Miller said. "Since Salomon has now passed, I'm the one in charge. And to answer your question, the chopper won't be here for a couple of days. We have to defend ourselves till then." He swallowed. As much as Jørn disliked the man, it was tough to see him so shaken.

"We don't know what this plant is capable of, and we can't run the risk of it getting off the continent. *Full* containment or hunting it are our only options. As badly as I want to research every inch of it, I would say full containment has been a spectacular failure. Killing it a must."

A few others began to shout unintelligibly.

"We cannot allow fear to rule us," Dr. Miller said. "It will drive us to madness. We need to stay calm and collected if we're to prevent the loss of any more lives.

"Now," he continued, "we all need dinner. After that, we'll set up a night-watch schedule. At any given time, a quarter of us will be awake to defend the rest of us if the monster shows up again. We stay together as a group."

TWENTY-FOUR:

Jørn was part of the first watch. He sat facing the door. A few other seed techs were awake to watch the vents. He held a fully fueled flamethrower in his hands.

Next to him, Lovise slept, her head in his lap. Elli was sleeping on the other side of the room, curled up in a thin blanket. He'd keep them both safe—the girl that made his heart flutter, and the girl who'd been a good friend to him.

A couple hours later, he woke Lovise for the second watch, and he fell asleep next to her. For a moment, he wished they were alone. But knowing that the Gnashvine was still out there was enough to dissuade him from acting on those thoughts.

He fell asleep and dreamed that Salomon was still alive and that the reinforcements showed up, and they finally defeated the Gnashvine.

—

He woke to the sound of a busy lab. Most people were up on their feet. The cooks were returning to the kitchen, accompanied by a group of armed seed techs. Despite the horrific events of the past couple of days, people still needed to eat.

"Hey, sleepyhead," Lovise said.

Jørn looked up. She was staring down at him, her brown eyes glimmering.

"Hi," he said, pushing himself up.

"How're you feeling?"

"I just want to go home," he said.

"You might be in luck." Lovise smiled. "You heard Dr. Miller, he got an ETA on the helicopter. We're getting out of here in a couple of days."

"That's too long!" Jørn said. "Way too long! They need to be here today! What are we supposed to do till then?"

"I can think of a lot of things." Lovise was still smiling. "But we should just focus on staying alive and killing that thing."

"If that's all we can do, then that's all we can do."

"Also, Miller thinks he knows where the Gnashvine is holed up. At least he has a theory about it."

Jørn ran a hand through his hair. "That's good. As long as we can keep track of the thing, then maybe we'll have a chance."

They sat in silence. Jørn didn't want to die. He didn't want anyone else to die. He succumbed to the notion that this was it—their only choice—and he was going to do all he could to survive. He grasped his axe and wrung the handle, thinking about the possibilities.

"So you grew up in Michigan," he said, cutting the silence.

Lovise eyed him, pursing her lips. "Is that a question?"

"No. I mean, you grew up in Michigan, then you lived in Connecticut when you went to Yale. Where are you going to live once we go back?"

She thought for a moment, but ultimately answered with a question. "Where are *you* going to go?"

"I was in Arizona before I came here," he said. "I'll head back to school to finish up."

"Well," Lovise said as she leaned in and kissed him on the cheek, "let's worry about it after we get out of here."

TWENTY-FIVE:

Once they had eaten a pancake and waffle breakfast—a surprisingly delicious, sugary meal–virtually everyone volunteered to be part of Dr. Miller's extermination team. Miller's wound had healed, and he was more spry than the day before. He must've made it his personal mission to avenge everyone's death. Everybody wanted off the continent. And the faster the Gnashvine was killed, the sooner everyone could go home.

The plan was to move as a single unit through the entire AUCV, searching every room until they found it.

Jørn, Dr. Miller, and two other seed techs led the group. They first went to the hot greenhouse. As Dr. Miller pushed to open the door, Jørn pressed the flame-thrower into his shoulder and hovered his finger over the trigger.

The door didn't swing with ease, so Jørn put his shoulder on it and pushed with Dr. Miller. Something beyond gave, and a chlorophyll substance flowed from under the door. They immediately stepped back. Jørn dipped the toe of his boot into it, but nothing happened. It had a consistency of green maple syrup. He then pressed his palm against the door and gently pushed again. It opened easier.

"Something must've been blocking it," Dr. Miller said.

A bluish hue spilled into the hallway. Dr. Miller poked his head inside, looked around for a moment, and then leaned back out, swinging the door wide open as he did so.

The sight of the room was unsettling. There were no more plants. What had once been a luscious greenhouse was now an empty refrigerator. The beds where plants had grown were empty. The floor—which Jørn had failed to notice the first time he'd come here—was a giant grate with square tubs of water below.

"What happened to the plants?" a seed tech asked.

"The Gnashvine must've absorbed them or something," Jørn said. The thought of a larger version of the man-eating plant was horrifying enough to make him shake the idea from his head and continue down the hallway.

As they moved farther, something in his gut told him that they'd find the Gnashvine in the cold greenhouse. And it wasn't just a feeling. It was also logic, since it wasn't in the hot greenhouse, and no matter how much a plant was genetically modified, it would always be drawn to an environment where it was created, and that was the cold.

He reached for the handle to the greenhouse. His hand shook slightly. But he had a flamethrower, a powerful one. And everyone else was armed with flamethrowers, knives, axes, or homemade weapons.

He opened the door.

Before he had time to raise his weapon, his suspicions were confirmed.

The room was crawling with plants. Vines snaked along the wall, and drooping leaves hung from the ceiling. Stalks and stems and branches covered the floor. Every few feet, the plant hive grew high like young trees.

Jørn looked through the grates to the water below. Plants grew there too. Everywhere he looked was green. Not only that, but the greenery was also *moving*. It was like he was watching the plant growing in real time.

"Its core has to be in here," he said.

"Do you see it?" Dr. Miller asked.

Jørn shook his head. "But the—"

Something slammed into his stomach. He dropped the flamethrower and stumbled back, disoriented. Gasping for air, he looked down, and a silent scream left his mouth.

A thick vine was wrapped around his stomach, squeezing tighter and tighter.

Dazed, winded, and terrified, he reached for the flamethrower, but the plant lifted him into the air and dragged him into the greenhouse. He slammed against a wall and fell to the grated walkway.

Below, through the grates' slats, Jørn watched as plants began moving together, merging into an unidentifiable shape in the water.

The Gnashvine formed right below him.

Jørn scrambled to his feet and looked at the door. Dr. Miller, Elli, Lovise, Rutger, and a handful of seed techs stepped forward. The monster plant didn't go for him, but instead slithered toward the door. Jørn back stepped as the Gnashvine thrust a hairy tendril into the actuator button, closing the door and destroying the button, leaving it and Jørn alone in the cold greenhouse.

TWENTY-SIX:

Jørn ran forward. A dozen vines slithered all around him, moving about like eels. Sharp spikes extended from their surfaces. He looked for a weapon, something sharp, anything to defend himself with, but if there had been anything, it was now buried in vines.

An enormous waxy leaf whipped out and swept his feet. He collapsed to the grates, grunting. Below him, the Gnashvine seemed to look at him from the depths of the water.

Pushing himself to his feet again, he bolted once more for the door. Vines swiped at him, but he jumped them each time. He reached the door and barreled into it, but it didn't budge.

"Please open. Please open. Please open." He kicked the door, but again it didn't move. On the other side, people shouted and banged on it.

Jørn turned around. More vines had appeared. They were moving toward him slowly as if waiting for a perfect opportunity to strike. He froze, an idea occurring to him.

Nearest to him, a red flowery vine with thorns reared back and then shot forward, its pointed tip headed straight for him. At the last moment, he leaped out of the way. The vine crashed into the door, breaking it off its hinges and sending it sailing into the hallway.

Dr. Miller reacted instantly from the threshold. He pressed the trigger on his flamethrower, sending bulbous blasts of fire into the greenhouse.

The vines snapped back, hissing. A few seed techs followed Dr. Miller, bearing their own weapons.

In the opening to the hallway, Elli appeared, two flamethrowers in hand.

"Here," Jørn said, holding his hand out.

She gasped when she saw him, but handed over his flamethrower. "I thought you were dead."

"Unfortunately," Jørn said, "I *plant* to be around for a long time." He turned away from Elli and stepped up beside Dr. Miller. The three seed techs behind them hacked away at some of the smaller vines while Dr. Miller kept blasting any of the larger ones that got too close.

"Be careful," Jørn said. "The Gnashvine is right below us."

As if on cue, a giant blackening vine broke through the floor, wrapped around one of the seed techs' waists, and yanked him through the floor.

Dr. Miller shouted, reaching for the tech, but it was futile. Below them, he was already being ripped apart and devoured by the hulking mass of plants and human meat.

Jørn fired at the dozen massive vines before them.

Dr. Miller pointed at the ground and pulled his trigger. Flames shot through the grating, engulfing the Gnashvine almost entirely. The greenhouse exploded in echoing hisses and reverberating shrieks.

Something dangled from the ceiling. It looked like a green sac, like a piece of the plant had fallen away from whatever it had been attached to.

Somebody grabbed Jørn's wrist and yanked him back. At that moment, the sac exploded. Seeds shot out in every direction, pelting Dr. Miller and the two remaining seed techs. Immediately, they began to scream. The seeds burned through their clothes and their skin.

More people spilled into the greenhouse. They carried flamethrowers, knives, and buckets of pesticides.

Chaos erupted. The thick vines ripped through the crowd of people, tearing straight through some of them. Darts shot out of plants clinging to the walls, piercing the skin of even more people. More pod sacs exploded, and people screamed as their skin burned. Flames were sprayed from flamethrowers, but the plants were quicker, effectively evading the attacks.

Jørn fired at a nearby vine, and it caught fire, flailing and shrieking. Elli pointed her flamethrower at another part of the Gnashvine, but something dark and green shot out of the chaos and ripped the flamethrower from her hand. She pulled out a long knife and began hacking at anything green.

Somebody screamed as they were yanked through the grates and into the Gnashvine's burning mass. Dr. Miller was still spraying flames at it, shouting as smoke from the acidic seeds curled away from his body.

Jørn tripped over a body missing a face, and before he could get back up, something popped, and a giant cloud of gray dust appeared.

No. Not dust. It was pollen.

Jørn began coughing violently. It was too thick, coating his throat and his lungs, suffocating him more effectively than smoke from any fire. Around him, others began coughing too.

Pollen, he thought. *How do we combat pollen?*

The vents whirred to life, and the pollen began to thin out. Another set of darts flew across the room. One pricked Jørn's neck, embedding in deep. He winced, cursing as he pawed at the end of it.

"Jørn!"

Somehow, Elli's voice reached him amidst the chaos. He turned, blinking rapidly, searching for her familiar face amongst the onslaught of violence. "Elli!"

"Jørn!"

He pushed past one seed tech who was missing an arm, and another who was holding a vine in his hand and repeatedly stabbing it.

"Jørn!"

He spotted her just a few yards away. A thinner vine was wrapped around her middle. It tried to pull her through a hole in the floor, but she had her hands firmly wrapped around a railing.

Without thinking, he ran forward, sending a blast of flames at the vine. It shrieked as it caught fire, but didn't let go.

Elli cried, great loud sobs that sounded like whimpers compared to the screaming and the carnage.

"I've got you," Jørn said, reaching out and grabbing her arm. "You're going to be okay!"

He stared into her eyes. What he saw, no words could describe. Her pupils were dilated, dark holes of fear. Time stopped, and a single tear welled up in the corner of her eye and dropped into the water. He squeezed her arm tighter, then he pulled. "I'm not going to let you—"

The next words never left his mouth. Something pulled on his ankle, and he crashed to the floor. Elli screamed as the vine made one final tug. Her hands slipped, the Gnashvine dragged her through the hole in the floor, and Jørn was left only staring after her.

He slid along the floor as the plant wrapped around his foot continued to pull him. He kicked and flailed, trying to escape its grasp, but to no avail.

Something gleamed in the corner of his vision, and an

axe fell just near his foot, severing the vine. He looked up. Lovise stood above him. She bled from multiple wounds, and she'd shed her coat. Now she wore a white tank top covered in dirt and blood.

"Fall back!"

It was Dr. Miller's voice. The remaining people in the greenhouse began moving toward the doors. Lovise offered her hand and pulled Jørn to his feet.

"Elli," he said, pointing to the hole in the floor.

"I know," Lovise said. "It's a bloodbath in here and we need to go."

TWENTY-SEVEN:

They sat huddled in the lab. The Gnashvine, it seemed, was content on staying in the greenhouse for now.

Jørn sat wrapped in a blanket, a slight shake to him. A quick glance around showed him that everyone was shaking. They'd just witnessed the violent murders of many of their colleagues.

"All in all," Dr. Miller said, his speckled beard still mottled with blood, "we may not have enough people."

Jørn wasn't sure how many people the AUCV employed. They'd lost a lot in the last two days and their numbers were dwindling.

Lovise sat next to him. Like several others, she'd shed her clothes since they were covered in blood and sat in her underwear, protected only by a thin blanket.

Elli . . .

Jørn couldn't shake the image of her getting yanked through the floor. It was like a relentless, visceral, repeating memory that made him want to vomit.

"We need to blow this place up," someone said.

Dr. Miller waved his hand. "Then we'll all freeze to death. They're not here to pick us up for the next few days."

"Then call the national guard," someone else argued.

"We can't give the plant a way off this continent. Seeds

or pollen! Imagine the catastrophe that would ensue if it reached the mainland."

"They'll come with weapons," someone else said. "Reinforcements will be able to help us kill it."

"We don't know that for sure," Dr. Miller said.

As people continued arguing with him, Jørn tried to keep his thoughts busy on the solution. Science, biology, it was proof that everything had a beginning and an end, that problems had solutions. Only a few questions in the scientific community had remained unanswered since their inception, but they were undoubtedly bigger than "how do we kill a plant?"

"What are you thinking?" Lovise asked. She scooted closer to Jørn.

"How we can kill it," he said.

"Do you have any ideas?"

He shook his head. Dozens of them had rushed the Gnashvine and thrown blades, fire, and pesticides at it to no avail. If there was a solution, it was far bigger than the weapons they had at their disposal.

"We can go try to find something," Lovise said.

"You mean leave the group full of tense, arguing, traumatized people?"

She nodded, smiling slightly.

"I don't think I've heard a better idea before," he said.

Jørn stood and almost collapsed under his own weight. Lovise grabbed him, and he leaned against a lab table. "Wow! My ankle is out of whack," he said, rolling it side to side to try to determine the damage. He slid his pant leg up to examine the injury. His calf and ankle were definitely swollen.

"We can stay here," Lovise said.

"I'll be okay. We have to find something to eradicate this thing."

They were alone in the maintenance room. No one had challenged them when they'd left the lab, and no one had followed them either. At this point, Jørn figured the other employees looked at him as a man in charge—Salomon and Dr. Miller had come to him with questions and concerns and generally always kept him by their sides. Even Dr. Miller hadn't shot them a questioning glance as they'd left.

They're probably thinking Lovise and I want to be alone, he thought.

Lovise lazily walked the room's perimeter, half-heartedly searching for anything of use. Jørn went to the center of the room and tore the tarp off the boring drill. It wasn't as large as he thought. But it was used to bore the majority of the tunnel hallways that the AUCV was built into. He estimated it could carry six people at a time if they all piled on the back. Two people could fit in the cab and two on each step on either side. He leaned forward, reading some information stickered to the cabin's glass.

"This is ballistic glass?" he asked, pointing to the boring drill.

"Yeah," Lovise said. The blanket was still wrapped around her shoulders. Jørn caught glimpses of blood on her chest.

"That means the cabin is virtually impenetrable from the outside," he said. "We could drive this into the greenhouse and drill through the Gnashvine."

"I don't think that would kill it," she said. "Plus, there's no way those walkways over the water would hold its weight."

"Maybe not kill it," he agreed, "but separate it into more manageable, killable pieces."

"Hmm," she said. "I can't see why Dr. Miller would be opposed to that. But we should run it by him. We would have to lure it out into the open tunnel first."

Jørn nodded. "That could work."

Something scraped near the door to the maintenance room.

Lovise jumped behind Jørn, and he took a step backward.

They'd accidentally left the door open, and now someone stood in its frame. They were silhouetted against the poor lighting, but the wrong parts of their body slumped, as if they'd just been terribly injured, and they wouldn't be able to stand for much longer.

"Can we help you?" Jørn asked.

The figure groaned and stepped into the light.

"Salomon," Lovise whispered.

TWENTY-EIGHT:

Salomon looked like the walking dead. His mouth hung open, and his body slumped to the left. His intestines hung out of the giant crimson slit through his abdominal muscle.

"Salomon," Jørn said. His instincts told him to move forward, to help, or to at least comfort this man in his last moments, but something else held him back.

"We thought you were dead," Lovise said.

"No," Salomon croaked, blood dribbling down his chin. "Please . . . take this." With a shaking hand, he lifted a vial into view.

Jørn squinted, but Lovise could already make it out. "Seeds?" she asked.

"The same ones that grew in Goran's head," Salomon said. "Seeds from the Gnashvine."

"What do you want us to do with it?" Jørn asked.

"Take them to the mainland," Salomon said in his raspy, dead-tired voice. "They must be studied. Learn about the plant to be able to kill it."

"Salomon," Lovise said, taking one small step forward, "I don't think that's such a good idea."

He slumped forward.

"I have a bad feeling about this," Jørn said.

Something slithered in the darkness of the doorway,

and then Salomon lethargically rose into the air. His body stiffened, as if all his muscles tightened at once, and then he was hovering four feet off the ground. He floated forward into the light. A thick, slimy vine extended from a hole in his back. His lips dripped with a mix of blood chlorophyll. Small pinky-sized plant tendrils flicked from inside his mouth.

Lovise gasped at the sickening sound. Plant and man as one organism was before them.

Salomon lurched forward. The plant vine thrust its puppet directly at Jørn.

Jørn jumped out of the way and rolled across the floor. Salomon, or Gnashvine-Salomon, followed him, arms swinging out at awkward angles, hands grasping empty air, dead eyes rolling uselessly in his skull.

Lovise went to the far wall, where she grabbed a flamethrower and spun. The blanket fell to the permafrost floor and she stood in bra, underwear, and combat boots. Her bare skin smeared with blood gave her a fierce look in the lambent light. She fired without hesitation, shooting a stream of flame directly at Gnashvine-Salomon.

Salomon shrieked, and the vine yanked him back, dodging the hot blaze. Jørn rolled again to avoid the flames.

A series of smaller vines burst out of the opening in Salomon's exposed innards and lashed out at Lovise. A few managed to cut her arms, but she pulled away before they could grab her.

"I'm sick of this!" she yelled, pressing the trigger once more.

The flamethrower exploded. Lovise was thrown against the side of the boring drill and collapsed in a heap on the ground. The rest of the explosion caught the out-reaching vines and spread to Salomon. He immediately went up in flames, screeching and flailing.

Jørn ran past the enflamed Gnashvine-Salomon, scooped Lovise into his arms, moved to the other side of the boring drill, and climbed inside. Once they were clear of the door, he shut and locked it.

Outside the maintenance room, Salomon writhed, the Gnashvine rolling his body on the ground to try and douse the flames.

Lovise whimpered.

"Are you all right?" Jørn asked.

"I think so," she said, wincing. "What happened?"

"The flamethrower exploded. I think one of the vines must have pierced the gas tank without me realizing."

"No, I mean, what happened with Salomon?"

"Oh," Jørn said. "I don't know. I guess the Gnashvine can control people like puppets. Controlling their voice box to make them speak."

"This is beyond belief," Lovise said. "Like, movie-level ridiculous. Are we dreaming? Was there a gas leak, and we're all high?"

"Unfortunately, I don't think so."

They paused. This was the closest they'd been since the day before. Lovise's hand was on his bare chest, and she shivered. Jørn's mind kept flashing back to that incredible moment, then to present. Lovise was sitting half-naked on his lap, her skin covered in blood and bruises, her hair a charred, matted mess, her eyes brimming with the constant tears the last few days had forced out of everyone. If they got out of this, he hoped she wouldn't be forever traumatized.

"This sucks," she said, looking up at him.

The boring machine shuddered.

"What was that?" Jørn whispered, holding a finger

up to his lips. Then something clanged against the boring drill, ramming it with full force. He looked around frantically, but it became very clear what was happening.

Vines snaked up around the cabin. The glass surrounding them cracked as the Gnashvine worked to crush the machine's cab.

"Turn it on!" Lovise yelled.

Jørn reached for the key in the ignition, but it wouldn't turn. As more and more vines began surrounding them, he frantically searched for an instruction manual on how to work the machine. He'd been in heavy equipment before, and almost always, they had simple directions for the driver. Finally, he found it.

"Move," Jørn demanded as he reached for the safety bar. The drill wouldn't turn on until he'd secured himself in the seat. Lovise obeyed, contorting herself into an awkward position so he could strap himself in. Once he did, she worked to find a more comfortable position while he twisted the key, and the boring drill whirred to life.

Jørn pressed the gas pedal and, using a gear stick on his right, set the drill to its fastest setting.

A few seconds later, the machine lurched to life, and they began moving forward at a snail's pace.

"Can it go any slower?" Lovise asked.

"Steer for me," Jørn said.

She grabbed the wheel and spun it to the left, so they were facing the door. In the few moments they'd spent inside the machine, the Gnashvine had covered the entire maintenance room in vines. They slithered along the walls and the ceiling, reaching for the drill. Glancing forward, Jørn saw that the drill wasn't yet spinning—the Gnashvine had wound its limbs entirely around it, successfully jamming it.

The machine stalled, and then with a quick surging of the vines, the drill was ripped off the front of the machine.

"We need to bail," he said.

"We'll never get out of here alive."

"We either face certain death in here or a possible chance of escape out there."

Lovise met his eyes, clearly terrified, kissed him on the lips, then began kicking at the boring drill's door.

TWENTY-NINE:

After a few kicks, the vines moved away just enough that the door flung open. Without wasting a second, Lovise and Jørn jumped out of the cabin and bolted for the exit. The vines had yet to cover the floor, but as they ran for the door, the vines on the walls flung out toward them.

They ducked and dodged. One of the vines managed to wrap Jørn's arm, but he yanked on it so hard that it ripped in half and then fell limp to the floor.

His heart was thrumming in his chest. An ominous feeling—one that told him he wouldn't make it out of the AUCV alive—suffocated all other thoughts. But he pushed forward anyway. Even if he didn't survive, maybe he could somehow save Lovise.

They jumped out of the maintenance room and immediately turned for the lab. Jørn relaxed, hopeful that they would make it out. The Gnashvine had to have a weakness; they had just not discovered it.

They ran for the stairs leading to the walkway. Behind them, vines and tendrils exploded out of the maintenance room, speeding toward Jørn and Lovise. To their left, the door to the AUCV loomed large.

"We're not gonna make it," she said between breaths.

Something scratched the back of Jørn's leg. He shoved

Lovise forward, and then his feet were yanked out from under him.

Slimy, heavy tendrils immediately wrapped him in a tight grip. He panicked, flailing, but to no avail. He was trapped, held tight by the vines. Every instinct in him begged him to flee, but he couldn't escape.

"Jørn!" Lovise screamed. She had stopped running, and while the plants were moving slower than before, they were still approaching her.

"Run!" he gasped. "Go!"

She was crying. He could see that much. But his death would mean nothing if she didn't escape, and part of her must have understood that because seconds later, she disappeared up the staircase leading to the lab.

Imminent death wasn't as terrifying as Jørn had imagined. He found that in these last moments, he'd already made his peace with the world. He'd been a good son, a good friend, a good student. He'd gotten the opportunity to see the inside of the AUCV, and while he really had done no studying there, he *had* seen what was possibly the world's first man-eating plant. Maybe they would make a musical about this place someday. *Little Shop of Horrors 2.0?* Probably, he realized as the vines squeezed the life out of him, giving the monstrous plant the name Gnashvine wasn't appropriate. Probably, Audrey III was much better.

"Audrey the Third," he whispered with his last breaths, seeing how it rolled off the tongue.

Yeah. That was much better than Gnashvine.

He closed his eyes, welcoming his death. One thought kept him happy: At least he hadn't been ripped apart like the others.

"Jø . . . ørn . . ."

He opened his eyes. The plants had relinquished their grip ever so slightly. He could breathe again.

The corpse of Salomon, or Gnashvine-Salomon, or Audrey Salomon III, stood in front of him. His face was scorched. White accordion cartilage vibrated as the plant tried to work Salomon's windpipe. Part of his throat lay exposed. Inside, tiny plant stalks moved about. Though he couldn't make out the details, Jørn realized that was how the Gnashvine was making Salomon talk—the plant was manipulating his vocal cords.

How smart is this thing? he wondered. *And where did it come from?*

"You must get these to the mainland," plant-Salomon said, his voice croaking and breaking in and out. He held up the vial once more.

"You'll have to kill me," Jørn spat. "You're never getting out of this vault."

"Do as I command!" Salomon ordered. "Or I'll crush every bone in your body."

Jørn smiled.

Was he really having a conversation with a plant? If this whole scenario ever hit headline news, mechanobiology would explode. Every young, impressionable biologist would want to be like him.

Salomon looked up, bits of flesh falling from his charred face.

Jørn's heart swelled as he heard a sound. Someone was here for him. He would still probably die, but at least he wouldn't die alone.

Craning his neck around, he saw Dr. Miller standing at the top of the steps. He held a flamethrower and sported a determined frown.

Gnashvine-Salomon made an odd clicking noise. Dr.

Miller began his descent down the steps. "You okay, kid?" he asked, looking at Jørn.

"Better than ever," he groaned.

"I'll do everything in my power to not let you infest the mainland," Dr. Miller said. "And that includes calling off the helicopters and staying here until every last one of your seeds is ash."

Salomon's corpse perked up. Jørn watched in horror, his gut sinking to his feet, as the vine connected to Salomon's back detached itself, and Salomon took two steps forward on his own.

"A plant reanimating a corpse," Dr. Miller said. And for the first time Jørn had seen, he smiled.

Salomon screeched, then lunged forward. His legs ran stiff, and his arms swung wildly by his sides. He looked like a puppet being controlled by a child.

Dr. Miller pressed the trigger on the flamethrower. As pure fire and heat blasted out the end, he ran forward, spraying at Salomon. The Gnashvine reared back. Dr. Miller didn't slow. Once Salomon had retreated near the back wall, Dr. Miller turned and shot flames at the vines holding Jørn. They fell away instantly, and Jørn collapsed.

"Th-thank you," he stuttered, his lips dry and his heart thudding. "I thought I was dead."

"Don't mention it," Dr. Miller said.

At that moment, a long and sharp spike pierced Dr. Miller through the back.

Jørn gasped and staggered away. The tip of the spike was showing through Dr. Miller's sternum. He looked down in disbelief, dropped the flamethrower, and fell to his knees. Blood poured out both sides of his body. He looked up at Jørn, a sense of surprise still evident in his eyes.

"Get . . ." he gasped. "Get everyone . . . outside."

The vine coursed up. Dr. Miller's eyes widened just before it thrust into his mouth.

Then he collapsed in a puddle of his own blood.

Dead.

THIRTY:

Jørn screamed.

The blood, the gore, the death he'd seen, it was finally all settling in. The shock that had covered him like a blanket ever since watching Goran and Kennet get ripped to shreds finally lifted, and it all hit Jørn with the force of a train.

He tried to run, but merely stumbled. He heard the vines slithering around him, but he didn't see them. His vision was blurring, fuzzing, and the air around him felt dense.

Something snatched his ankle once again. He tried fighting free, but it felt like he was moving through sand. His movements were too slow, too weighed down.

The vines curled around him once more. This was it. Lovise was gone. Everyone must've been in the lab. Dr. Miller was dead. And he was alone.

From across the room, Gnashvine-Salomon approached him, walking like both his knees were breaking.

As the vines tightened around Jørn, crushing his rib cage, he gasped for one last breath.

Something revved in the distance. It sounded like an engine, like one that belonged to a motorcycle. Maybe heaven was a lot more like life than people theorized. Or maybe this had all been a terrible dream, and he was really asleep in his old dorm, and the sounds of a busy street in the early morning were waking him up.

Something flashed by. The vines around him slackened.

He opened his eyes all the way, willing his vision to clear. In front of him, a trail of vines lay crushed and splintered on the ground in green puddles of chlorophyllic goop. And a few feet from him, Salomon was flattened on the ground, his arms raised like roots from an upturned tree, twisted and bent.

The sound of the motor broke through the shock, and Jørn glanced over to see a snowmobile race along more vines, splitting them in half, then driving straight over Salomon's head.

Instantly, Salomon's corpse went limp. The vines in the room began to retreat.

A plume of flames sent more vines reeling away. Darts, smaller versions of the one that had killed Dr. Miller, shot out from the unseen edges of the room.

The snowmobile turned and zoomed past Jørn. Before he could react, the driver grabbed him by his shirt and yanked him onto the back of the seat.

All Jørn saw was shoulder-length blonde hair.

He peered closer. Behind it was a slender neck of milky-smooth skin.

"Elli," he whispered, his adrenaline transforming into a wave of relief.

Elli turned to face him. A few gashes lined her face, and she was bleeding from her eyebrow.

"H-how?" he asked.

"Not now," she said. She lifted the front of the snowmobile as they reached the staircase, and it raced up the steps. Jørn held tight as the vehicle jostled below him.

He glanced behind. The vines snaked after them.

There were so many—thousands. The sight made him nauseous.

Elli turned the snowmobile down the walkway and revved the engine. It shot toward the lab. The greenhouses flung past them, and then she brought the snowmobile to a stop, jumped off, grabbed Jørn by the hand, and ran into the lab.

The survivors were gathered in a clump near the center of the room. They bore weapons of all kinds—some carried stakes sharpened from chair legs, others held knives from the kitchen and flamethrowers from the maintenance room, some gripped bottles of chemicals, glass shards attached to the tip of long poles, and strands of rope that were pierced through with sharp objects.

"Jørn!" It was Lovise. She broke from the crowd, tackled him to the ground, and kissed him. She now wore pants and a heavy coat. Her lips tasted salty, like sweat. "I thought you were dead," she whispered as she continued to kiss him.

"Almost," he said.

Lovise smiled and climbed off him, then helped him to his feet with one hand.

"We soaked the lab in pesticides," Elli said. "Hopefully, it holds the Gnashvine off for a few minutes."

Jørn stepped away from Lovise and approached her.

"I tried to save you," he whispered.

"I know," she said.

"How did you survive?"

"I got pulled under, and some vines held me down, but the Gnashvine was too busy trying to kill all of you, so I managed to cut myself free and climb into a vent. I hid there until I was sure nothing was coming after me, and then I slowly made my way through the vents until I found all of them sitting in the lab."

Despite the madness and the slaughter of the last couple of days, his heart was full. His friend had survived what was meant to be certain death.

"And the snowmobile?" he asked.

"One of the techs found a few in a storage area down the hall. Along with that." She pointed to a pile of boxes near the group of people.

"TNT," Lovise explained, sidling up next to Jørn.

"Nobody had any clue it was here," Elli said. "Probably for good reason. But we assume Salomon and Dr. Miller knew about it. I think it was left here in case we got caved in—then if we had to, we could blow our way out of here."

"So what's the plan?" Jørn asked.

"Dr. Miller gave us some orders before he went to save you two," Elli said. She looked tired. The hopeful, optimistic smile she'd arrived with was now an uncertain, concerned frown. He wished he could change that for her.

"He told us to get outside and blow up the whole thing."

"But we'll freeze to death out there," Jørn said.

"His last request was that we trust him," Lovise said. "Besides, it's either risk our chances with the weather or with the monster that will eat us."

"Okay," Jørn said with absolutely not an ounce of faith. He looked ahead. Standing before him was a group of nurses, janitors, chefs, and a bunch of nerdy scientists. Along with the makeshift weapons they held, they wore their warmest clothes. It wasn't precisely an army fit for battle, but at least they were something.

"Where can I get a coat?" he asked.

THIRTY-ONE:

Half an hour later, once a few of the seed techs had brought all three snowmobiles inside, Jørn sat on the back of one. They'd spent most of that time devising a plan, and everyone waited to carry it out.

Elli was driving a snowmobile with a seed tech on the back. Jørn had opted to ride with Lovise and had his arms wrapped around her waist. One of his hands gripped her wrist, and in his other hand, he held five sticks of TNT wrapped together with a fuse sticking out the top.

Unable to return to his room and retrieve his arrival clothes, he was thankful he'd found warm pants and a huge coat. No one was certain how long they'd be able to survive outside, but everybody was dressing warm to ensure they had at least more than a few hours.

Rutger manned the third snowmobile, with a familiar-looking cook on the back, and two seed techs, a man and a woman, were on the other one.

Jørn looked over his shoulder to where the rest of the survivors stood. They still held their weapons, but some also held sticks of TNT. They'd decided everybody would deposit the TNT where they saw fit, and then Jørn would be the one to light his first. While they had no idea if it would set off the rest of the TNT, they could only hope.

All they had were scraps for a plan, and they just had to pray it would turn out to be a whole meal.

"Once we leave," Elli said loud enough for them all to hear, "everyone wait here for one minute, then make a break for the door. Hopefully, by then, we'll have it open."

"Aye, aye," someone said.

Lovise turned to face Jørn while she had the chance and he winked. She smiled half-heartedly at him. He wanted to think about his future with her, but he couldn't allow himself to think that far ahead. He needed to focus on the here and now. Factoring in their chances of success was foolish. It would only give him more nerves.

"Three!" Elli shouted. "Two!"

The snowmobiles' engines roared to life. Jørn leaned into Lovise. "Put the *petal to the metal*," he whispered.

He swore he felt her roll her eyes, but in a happy, flirty way.

"One!" she shouted.

And they were off.

The moment they broke into the hallway, the vines descended on them like snow in a blizzard. The snowmobile was moving too fast for any of them to grab hold, but Jørn ducked his head anyway. Behind him, the other three snowmobiles followed.

Lovise veered the vehicle to the left and careened it down the stairs. He held tight, wincing as he temporarily lifted on the seat and then came smashing down.

Lovise curved back to the cafeteria in an effort to draw some of the Gnashvine away. It worked. The vines followed them. Jørn did his best to look around, but all he saw were the AUCV and the vines. The Gnashvine, if its giant human/plant amalgam form still existed, was nowhere to be seen.

The other three snowmobiles went toward the door leading out of the AUCV. Hopefully, they would get it open in time.

The vines lashed out at them, their outsides coated in chlorophyll. Some were covered in barbs, others in spikes, and some had rows of what appeared to be teeth surrounding them. Lovise spun the snowmobile around, brought it to a halt, lifted her flamethrower, and fired at the plants.

A burst of static exploded across the speaker system. Then, seconds later, the familiar riffs of AC/DC's *Back in Black* began to play.

While devising their plan, they'd decided the best thing they could do to help their chances against the Gnashvine was to control as much chaos as possible.

The vines fidgeted for a moment, swinging this way and that with the music. Jørn reached forward and twisted the snowmobile's handle slightly. It moved forward. Lovise continued shooting plumes of flames at the plants, and slowly they drove them back.

Ahead, Jørn noticed the other snowmobiles were gone. He panicked for a split second, terrified that the Gnashvine had gotten to them, but then noticed the door to the waiting room was open. Hopefully, they'd get the giant vault-like door open next.

Gray dust filled the air. The Gnashvine had deployed its pollen again. Jørn and Lovise took a deep breath, and then she dropped the flamethrower and sped forward.

The vines shrieked as they ran them over, and poison darts zoomed past their heads. Jørn's vision went gray when they passed through the pollen, but he unwrapped one arm from around Lovise and rubbed his eyes until they were clear again.

They emerged into a battlefield. The other survivors

had arrived, swinging, hacking, and shooting flames at the vines that whirled around them.

One vine grabbed Jørn around the arm, but a random seed tech appeared and sliced it in half. He was grateful that the cut was all plant and not his arm. Everything was happening so fast. So chaotic. Another reached for Lovise, and she set it on fire with a quick blast from her flamethrower.

A wave of frigid air washed through the whole building.

Jørn's heart skipped a beat. His skin grew hot. Elli was quicker and opened the door.

"Everybody out!" she shouted.

Lovise revved up the snowmobile and drove for the exit. People ran after them, leaving some of their colleagues ripped in half, stabbed through the hearts, and strangled to death behind them. Jørn looked away. He couldn't see any more of it.

The door to the waiting room loomed nearer and nearer, and then Lovise sped the snowmobile through.

Where once the door to the AUCV had been, there was now a giant, gaping circle. Snow swirled outside, but Jørn barely noticed the biting temperature as they drove out into the white continent of Antarctica.

Lovise braked, and he jumped off the seat. From the entrance of the AUCV, the remaining survivors ran toward him, only eight in total. They'd lost so many people, but he couldn't think about that. Not yet. At least some of them had lived. And he had to keep it that way.

He ran against the flow of the screaming group. Hundreds of vines spilled out of the waiting door, filling it up so quickly that the entire wall cracked and fell into pieces.

Jørn reached into his pocket, his breath haggard, and

pulled out a lighter. He clicked it three times before it sparked to life. Then he lit the TNT.

He was still running, but he came to a stop only fifteen feet away from the entrance. From the ruins of the collapsed wall, the Gnashvine rose.

It was unrecognizable, a writhing mess of human limbs, vines, and roots. It stood at least twelve feet tall and moved about like a squid on dry land.

"There you are," Jørn said as the flame burned farther down the TNT's fuse.

He caught a glimpse of Salomon's face, crushed and flattened from where the snowmobile rolled back into the monster.

"I'm gonna kill you . . . *once and floral*," Jørn said. Then he threw the TNT.

He didn't watch it sail through the air, didn't wait to see if he hit the target. Instead, he turned and ran back to the snowmobile. Everybody ran past the platform where helicopters used to land to a slope on the other side. They were descending to safety.

But Lovise had waited for Jørn. He jumped on the back of the snowmobile, and she tore forward so fast that he nearly fell backward.

An explosion erupted behind them, and Jørn looked back just in time to see pieces of the Gnashvine flailing in the snow, burning to a crisp, eventually becoming as limp as a dead man.

More explosions followed in quick succession. About twelve in total. The earth shook. Lovise raced forward.

"There's gonna be an avalanche," Jørn said, the realization dawning on him with a weighty terror.

"I know," Lovise said. But she offered no words above that.

And then, as if it were a trick of the light, something flashed in front of the faraway sun.

Jørn looked up.

Ten helicopters descended toward them, their blinking lights the most beautiful things Jørn had ever seen.

EPILOGUE: THREE MONTHS LATER...

Exactly twelve weeks following the mysterious and tragic accident at the Avling Universal Crop Vault in Antarctica, details are still obscure. The survivors, nine in total, have yet to make a public appearance beyond their televised arrival in Chile. Thus far, those left behind have been confirmed dead. Friends and families are left confused and frustrated as the world's governments refuse to divulge any further details. The President of the United States issued only one remark about the incident, citing it as "tragic" and "concerning."

The public continues to demand answers, though some insiders claim we may never get them, chalking up the incident to a conspiracy designed to ignite a world war. Despite these claims, the United Nations has scheduled a press conference for this week. It is expected they will discuss what many people have labeled The Antarctic Massacre.

Jørn set the paper down on his counter, then thought better of it and tossed it in the trash.

It'd been three months since the helicopters had picked them all up from the AUCV. He looked into the mirror hanging on the wall and straightened his tie. He was still covered in scratches, though they were fading fast.

In an effort to keep them silent and avoid public lawsuits, the government had offered each of the survivors a massive sum of money, with earnings paid out when they were cleared in a military base of all plant pollen and seeds. They didn't want some sort of chlorophyllin contagion to get into the water or spread to the population. With only a portion of it, Jørn had purchased a house in Arizona, a hot climate that rarely saw snow and ice. He would do his best to enjoy the time he had off because in a few months, he knew he'd be forced, along with the rest of the survivors, to speak in front of all the governments.

He also suspected all of this would get out somehow. Elli was correct. An intense concentration of proton-heavy nuclei cosmic rays originating from outer space had traveled through the universe at nearly the speed of light, directly into the seed vault of the AUCV. Jørn had theorized that these specific cosmic particles were thought to originate from a supernova consisting of tightly woven neutron stars.

Over time, these rays mutated the seeds stored there, and that was what created the Gnashvine. He knew it! He could prove it in a lab setting! But for now, he buried the hypothesis and experiment design deep in his brain. Somebody somewhere would leak the true story of what happened, and then his life would become a series of interviews, TV specials, and case studies.

He shook his head, trying to clear his thoughts. While a plant surviving off blood not using natural photosynthesis to live would matter one day, none of it did now.

Only two things mattered right now. The first and foremost was healing. Every doctor he'd seen had prescribed him just that: "Rest up. Let yourself heal."

The second had to do with a girl.

He unhooked the keys to his brand-new car from the key ring on his wall, then went to his garage. He had a date; one he had promised to embark on a few months ago.

Finally, after what had happened in Antarctica, he could confidently tell Lovise he was absolutely not a Carpenter guy. More of a Craven. He had a feeling she'd say the same.

THE END

As a kid, Tyler H. Jolley always had a knack for storytelling. When he grew bored of old fables, he created his own exciting and unique worlds. Many years later, he still had so many new ideas and stories swirling in his head, but with nowhere to share it. That's when he put his pencil to paper and let the creative juices flow.

His debut novel, *Extracted*, came out in 2013 and swiftly became an Amazon Best Seller and Spencer Hill Press Best Seller. *Prodigal and Riven*, the second and third books in The Lost Imperials series were released in May of 2015.

After a brief hiatus he restructured and returned to writing. His Adventurous Ali series has received much praise. To date, he's released four in the series.

When he's not writing, you can find him at his orthodontic practice, mountain biking, or on the hunt for the perfect doughnut.

www.ingramcontent.com/pod-product-compliance
Lightning Source LLC
Chambersburg PA
CBHW021715190726
48289CB00008B/2544